THE
"CHRISTMAS CAROL"
TRIVIA BOOK

THE "CHRISTMAS CAROL" TRIVIA BOOK

EVERYTHING YOU EVER WANTED TO KNOW ABOUT EVERY VERSION OF THE DICKENS CLASSIC

Paul Sammon

A Citadel Press Book
Published by Carol Publishing Group

A Citadel Press Book
Published by Carol Publishing Group

Citadel Press is a registered trademark of Carol Communications, Inc.
Editorial Offices: 600 Madison Avenue, New York, NY 10022
Sales and Distribution Officies: 120 Enterprise Avenue, Secaucus, NJ, 07094
In Canada: Canadian Manda Group, PO Box 920, Station U, Toronto, Ontario M8Z 5P9
Queries regarding rights and permissions should be addressed to Carol Publishing Group, 600 Madison Avenue, New York, NY 10022

Carol Publishing Group books are available at special discounts for bulk purchases, sales promotions, fund-raising, or education purposes. Special editions can be created to specifications. For details, contact Special Sales Department, Carol Publishing Group 120 Enterprise Avenue, Secaucus, NJ 07094.

Manufactured in the United States of America

10 9 8 7 6 5 4 3 2 1

Library of Congress Cataloging-in-Publication Data

Sammon, Paul M.
      The "Christmas Carol" trivia book : everything you ever wanted to know about every version of the Dicks classic / by Paul Sammon.
          p. cm.
      "A Citadel Press book."
      ISBN 0-8065-1579-1 (paper)
      1. Dickens, Charles, 1812-1870. Christmas carol–Miscellanea. 2. Dickens, Charles, 1812-1870–Adaptations–Miscellanea. 3. Christmas stories, English–Adaptations–Miscellanea. 4. Christmas stories, English–Miscellanea. I. Title.
PR4572 . C7S26   1994
823'.8–dc20

p4-20516
CIP

For Alastair Sim
The Finest Scrooge of All

PHOTO CREDITS

ACKNOWLEDGMENTS

A number of individuals, institutions, and books helped make this modest volume a reality. Therefore, and with a toast of good Christmas cheer, Ye Author would like to thank:

Lori Perkins, Ye Author's agent, for shepherding the deal to fruition. Ye Author's editor, Keven McDonough, at the Carol Publishing Group, who first contacted him about the idea. Peter Ackroyd's definitive biography, *Dickens* (Harper Collins, 1990) was an invaluable research aid concerning A Christmas Carol's author and the story itself; Ye Author would also like to thank all those other writers whose own excellent works helped him collate some of the facts gathered herein (the reader is urged to consult the bilbliography at the back of this book for all reference works).

Further thanks to: Kathy Murray and T. E. D. Klein, for pointing out the "mirror gaffe" in Alastair Sim version: Sheri Wohl, manager, Entertainment

Publicity, CBS Television, New York, Leonard Maltin, for taking time out of his hectic schedule; Don Shay, publisher, Cinefex Magazine; Jerry Beck, for the Magoo pressbook: Baick Cotton at Buena Vista Home Video; Linda Jones, of Chuck Jones Film Productions, for her personal kindness and phtographic generosity; Barabara Dan a Tollis of the Lippin Group; Carol at Hanna-Barbera Productions; Clair, Donovan, and Heidi at Eddie Brandt's Saturday Matinee; Eric Caiden adn John Kantas at Hollywood Book and Poster; the hard-working staff of the Margaret Herrick Library Academy of Motion Picture Arts and Sciences; Lieth Adams at the Warner Brothers Corporate Archives; Alvin H. Marill, video-emeritus of made-for-televison material, for his diligence and addtions; and Andrew Milhan and Paul Lewis, for the information on the Long Beach dance production of A Christmas Carol—as well as for being the best neighbors Ye Author has ever had.

Finally, Ye Author would like to dedicate this book as a perpetual Christmas present to both his wife, Sheryl Edith Sires Sammon, and her side of the family (Ada, George, Connie, Jack, Kim, Bob, Kay, Azfar, Rick, Mary, Jennifer, Scott, Kevin, Andy, Emiuly, Abigail, Olivia, Ricky, Walker), and to Ye Author's own immediate relatives (Kay, Pat, and Mark).

God Bless You, Every One!

CONTENTS

INTRODUCTION

It has warmed the hearts of an entire world for over 150 years. It has been translated into as many languages as there are native tongues. It has spawned legions of theatrical, film and television adaptations.

There are even people who believe that it invented everything we hold dear about Christmas itself.

Its name?

A Christmas Carol.

A ghostly, uplifting Yuletide story by Charles Dickens that's among the most beloved and influential tales of the holiday season.

Since its initial publication in 1843, this classic story of a heartless miser's mircaculous conversion on Christmas Eve has evolved from popular success to folkore to myth. And the characters and story of *A Christmas Carol* are just as familiar to a child in Atlanta as to an adult in Russia: who hasn't heard of the

names Scrooge, Bob Crachit, or Tiny Tim? Or been enthralled by the mysticasl appearances of the Ghosts of Christmas Past, Christmas Present and Christmas Yet to Come?

Yet how much do *you* know about *A Christmas Carol?*

Really know?

About its author?   The original story? Or the dozens of *A Christmas Carol* adaptations, for films and television, that are now availabel on videocassette?

The "Christmas Carol" Trivia Book was expressly created to give you, the reader, the fullest opportunity to enjoy, examine and experience the many different facets which comprise Dickenss holiday gem.

Within these pages you'll find facts pertaining to the creation of the original *Chirstmas Carol* book. Relive the sometimes sade life of its creator. Discover behind-the-scenes information on more that sixty various *Christmas Carol* adaptations, ones done for film, television, and cartoons. There's even a chapter near book's end listing the various versions of *A Christmas Carol* now available on home video, along with information on how to order them.

Each chapter examines a separate aspect of the tale. Within that chapter you'll find pages of interesting information on different subjects, followed by trivia questions pertaining to those specific topics.

Yet while it's true that Ye Author has tried to be as comprehensive as possible, he makes no claims that his book is the last word on its subject. Quite the con-

trary, in fact.For this little volume, like *A Christmas Carol* itself, was written purely to entertain.

But now it's time to pull up an easy chair by a warm, roaring fire. To lean back and enjoy this affectionate excursion through a beloved holiday treat.

While we're at it, why not raise a glass of christmas cheer? As Tiny Tim himself so perfectly put it—

God bless us, every one!

THE "CHRISTMAS CAROL" TRIVIA BOOK

CHAPTER ONE
THE AUTHOR

CHARLES DICKENS

Charles Dickens's place in literary history would have been secure even if he hadn't written one of the greatest Christmas stories.

In addition to being England's greatest novelist, he was the most popular. During his adult years, a series of incredibly successful, socially conscious novels and short stories brought Charles Dickens wealth and worldwide celebrity, factors which led to a highly profitable series of lecture tours, magazine appearances, and newspaper interviews. Yet Dickens's early life was anything but happy. His childhood was marred by economic hardship, brushes with the law, and a constant series of moves from one squalid town to another, incidents which the great writer later used to lasting effect in his still-potent fictional works.

Born on the seventh of February 1812, on the outskirts of Portsmouth, England, Charles John Huffam Dickens entered life into a lower-middle-class family

Charles Dickens reading aloud, from the Illustrated London News, *March 19, 1870.*

that had recently been tainted by scandal. Only two years earlier, Charles Barrows, Dickens's maternal grandfather, had been discovered embezzling money from the English Navy pay office. In order to escape prosecution, Barrows then fled to the Isle of Man, marking Dickens's grandfather not only as a thief but a fugitive from justice as well.

Money problems and threats of legal action would dog the young Charles Dickens throughout his formative years. Mostly because of Dickens's father, John (a man whom the author both adored and despised, traits shown by Ebenezer Scrooge toward his *own* father). John Dickens was a Royal Navy pay clerk responsible for giving port workers and ship crews their wages. Unfortunately, and despite the fact that he routinely handled large amounts of cash, John's own fiscal sense was irresponsible in the extreme. He was constantly in debt. Borrowed recklessly and often. Heedlessly lived beyond his means. This meant that the Dickens family was forever obsessed with matters of security and financial stability.

By 1821, the full Dickens clan—which would eventually include, in addition to father John and mother Elizabeth, Charles's sisters Frances Elizabeth and Laetitia Mary, and brothers Frederick, Augustus, Alfred Lamert, and Alfred Allen (who died six months after birth)—had all moved to London. This vast, bustling metropolis made an indelible impression on the keenly observant young Charles, who was equally fascinated by both the grinding poverty he saw in the streets and the rowdy nightlife being celebrated in such squalid London slums as The Seven Dials.

Then, in the year 1824, two events occurred which would affect the budding novelist's life.

The first concerned putting the then twelve-year-old Charles to work. His first job was at Warren's Blacking House, an ancient, rotting, tumbledown London factory that manufactured boot blacking. Young Charles's duties lay in labeling bottles of this noxious substance; he worked ten dreary hours a day for the munificent sum of six or seven shillings a week (about thirty to thirty-five cents). Needless to say, such tedious, repetitive work was hardly a source of spiritual nourishment for this imaginative lad. As the author himself was to later write of this period, "My whole nature was . . . penetrated with . . . grief and humiliation."

1824 also saw a second momentous event, one that permanently terminated Dickens's childhood.

His father John, still mismanaging his money, had run up a debt of some forty pounds to a local baker named James Karr. When John couldn't pay this bill, he was incarcerated in London's Marshalsea Prison. This double calamity of forced child labor and a father being thrown into debtor's prison had a catastrophic effect on the young Charles. Not only had his family been torn apart; he was now working long, hard hours for a pittance.

Consequently, Dickens's days were filled with anxiety and dread. These twin emotions and memories would haunt the adult Charles for the remainder of his life.

Ye Author has taken the trouble of detailing Dickens's first twelve years

because they ultimately became the realistic grist to his artistic mill. For Charles's novels and short stories would obsessively return to the themes of his youth, to scenes of brutal child labor, poverty, and broken families, themes that struck a deep chord in the readers of his day.

But Dickens's *literary* career actually began rather modestly. Always entranced by literature and the theater (Dickens may have been an amateur actor early in life; historians disagree on this point), the young Charles nevertheless initially began his professional career as an office boy in a law firm. He next found employment as an independent shorthand court reporter, before becoming a reporter of parliamentary debates for the *Morning Chronicle* newspaper in 1835.

Dickens then wrote a series of satires on daily London life titled *Sketches by Boz* (his first pen name) for *Old Monthly Magazine*. When these satires met with popular approval, Charles was asked to do another series. He quickly churned out *The Posthumous Papers of the Pickwick Club*, better known today as *The Pickwick Papers*.

It was *The Pickwick Papers* that suddenly made Charles Dickens a success, at the age of twenty-four. Yet still goaded by the demons of his youth, Dickens refused to rest on his laurels. His famous, socially conscious novel *Oliver Twist* (1839), a grim story of orphans, child labor, and thieving street urchins, was greeted with wild enthusiasm. And over the next thirty years Dickens continued to produce masterworks of English literature: *Nicholas Nickleby* (1839), *The Old*

Curiosity Shop (1840), *David Copperfield* (1850), *A Tale of Two Cities* (1859), and *Great Expectations* (1861).

During this period Dickens became the world's first modern popular author, sort of a nineteenth-century Stephen King, a bestselling writer whose every word was devoured by critics and the public alike. Dickens also made successful lecture/reading tours of England and America, founded two weekly magazines (*Household Words* and *All the Year Round)*, and became a tireless social activist crusading against the indignities heaped upon the English poor.

On June 9, 1870, Charles Dickens was stricken with a paralytic stroke. He died in the dining room of Gad's Hill Place, a grand house which he'd first seen as a boy. (His own father had pointed it out to him as a child.) Dickens's last words were "On the ground."

News of his death traveled around the world. In America, the great poet Henry Wadsworth Longfellow wrote that "I never knew an author's death to cause such general mourning. It is no exaggeration to say that this whole country is stricken with grief."

Gone was the man who'd created such popular characters as Little Nell, Fagin, and Oliver Twist; no more would the world savor the adventures of benighted fictional creations like Pip of *Great Expectations*. Also gone was the possibility that Dickens should produce other popular works like *Cricket on a Hearth* (1845), a Christmas tale of a family cricket that chirps when all is well and is silent during

times of unhappiness.

The world had lost a true original, a man who, interestingly, was just as famed for Christmas stories such as *The Chimes, The Haunted Man, The Poor Relation's Story*, and *The Holly Tree* as for his best-known novels and among those novels was most beloved Christmas tale of them all—*A Christmas Carol*.

TRIVIA QUESTIONS

The questions in this chapter are probably the toughest in the book; most of these brainteasers can only be answered through a familiarity with Charles Dickens's work. Which in turn demands that you someday pick up and read a Dickens *book*. Don't worry, though. The questions aren't *that* hard.

Let's start with two easy ones. . .(Answers on page 209)

1. When was Charles Dickens born?

2. Where?

3. Name the villain of *Oliver Twist*.

4. Pick the actor who played the part of the villain in a hit 1968 British musical film adaptation of a famous Dickens novel. What was this film's title?

    a. Alan Bates—*Oliver!*   b. Peter O'Toole—*Oliver Twist*
    c. Oliver Reed—*Oliver!*   d. Alec Guinness—*Fagin*

Charles Dickens on his deathbed.

5. What was Charles Dickens's first job?

6. How old was he when he received his first employment?

7. Pick the publication dates of *A Tale of Two Cities* and *Great Expectations*.

   a. 1859–1861   b. 1861–1870   c. 1839–1843

8. Where was Dickens's father imprisoned for bad debts?

9. Who is the reclusive old woman who sets the plot in motion for *Great Expectations*?

10. Which of Dickens's brothers died at the age of six months?

11. Pick the name of Dickens's first great literary success:

    a. *David Copperfield*   b. *Oliver Twist*   c. *The Pickwick Papers*

12. To what seedy part of town was Dickens drawn when he first moved to London with his family?

13. Pick the name of Dickens's mother:

    a. Jean   b. Frances   c. Anna   d. Elizabeth   e. Anabella

14. What was Charles Dickens's first print-related job?

15. Name one Dickens Christmas story and Christmas *essay* other than *A Christmas Carol*.

16. For what publication did Dickens report on speeches of Parliament?

17. What was the Dickens family's greatest fear during Charles's childhood?

18. What was the full name of the heroine of *The Old Curiosity Shop*?

19. Many adaptations of *Great Expectations* have been filmed, but in what year was the version considered definitive released? Who was its director?

20. What was Dickens's greatest lifelong fear?

21. Pick the character who sacrifices himself for the good of others in *A Tale of Two Cities:*

    a. Charles Darnay   b. Sydney Carton   c. Stryver
    d. Alexander Manette   e. Malcolm DeFarge

22. In 1842, Dickens made a trip to America, where he caused a great commotion by demanding an end to slavery and the establishment of an international copyright. Name the two books Dickens wrote that subsequently reflected that trip.

    a. *Bleak House*   b. *Martin Chuzzlewit*   c. *Little Dorrit*
    d. *Dombey and Son*   e. *American Notes*

23. What were Dickens's last words?

24. Where did he die? When?

25. How much did Dickens earn per week for his first job?

26. What was the title of the novel Dickens was writing at the time of his death, one that remained unfinished?

27. Where is Dickens buried?

CHAPTER TWO

THE STORY

CREATING "A CHRISTMAS CAROL"

"Marley was dead: to begin with. There is no doubt whatever about that." Thus begins Charles Dickens's perennial holiday classic *A Christmas Carol*, which celebrated its 150th anniversary on December 19, 1993.

What a 150 years it has been! Since the day it was published, *A Christmas Carol* has entertained thousands of eager readers. Yet its plot is a fairly simple one; *A Christmas Carol* is a ghost story, one whose roots are found in the old English custom of telling supernatural stories during the Christmas season.

Its narrative?

On Christmas Eve, 1843, a miserly old moneylender named Ebenezer Scrooge—a man who hates Christmas and everything it stands for—is visited by the ghost of his dead partner, Jacob Marley. Marley warns Scrooge that on this single night he will be visited by three spirits. Their mission is to show Scrooge visions of Christmases past, present, and future, in an attempt to save Scrooge from the hellish afterlife to which Marley himself is condemned.

Marley vanishes. Beginning at one A.M., the Ghosts of Christmas Past, Present, and Yet-to-Come do indeed visit the old sinner, and Scrooge witnesses many glimpses of his life. He sees himself as a schoolboy, business apprentice, young lover. Is shown the joyous family life of his underpaid clerk, Bob Cratchit. Is warned that he will die, alone and despised, if he continues his wicked ways.

Suddenly, Scrooge awakens. It's a beautiful Christmas morning. Realizing he has wasted his life, the misanthropic old man is so thankful to have survived these terrible visions that his very nature changes. He now becomes cheerful and benevolent, a man who not only rescues Bob Cratchit's sickly son, Tiny Tim, from certain death, but forevermore holds the joy of Christmas in his heart.

That, in essence, is *A Christmas Carol.* And you'd be hard-pressed to find many people who don't know it.

In fact, many of its passages are so familiar that they recur with predictable regularity in every adaptation attempted by film or television. And since part of the fun of this book is recognizing the ways various adapters have included these passages in their own versions of Dickens work, Ye Author now presents a few familiar *Carolian* highlights. Try to remember these later on; you'll be surprised at how often they pop up throughout this book.

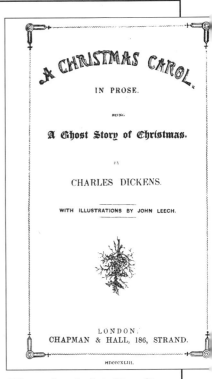

Title page from the first edition of A Christmas Carol.

❋ *Cratchit and the Coal Fire.* As he works in the bitterly cold offices of Scrooge & Marley, Bob Cratchit, Scrooge's put-upon employee, asks for more coal to help warm the room. His miserly boss refuses.

❋ *The Charity Seekers.* While working in his office on Christmas Eve, Scrooge is visited by two gentlemen seeking donations for the poor. Ebenezer refuses with this classic line: "Are there no poorhouses?" "Some of the poor would rather die than go there," one gentleman replies. "Then perhaps they should die," Scrooge shoots back, "and reduce the surplus population." This line will return to haunt Scrooge, when the Ghost of Christmas Present later uses the same words to respond to Ebenezer's question about the fate of Tiny Tim.

❋ *Nephew Fred.* Scrooge is visited by his young nephew, Fred, who invites the old miser to a party on Christmas day. Again, Scrooge refuses.

❋ *The Ghostly Doorknocker.* When Scrooge leaves his office to go home, the knocker on his front door (which is usually depicted as a lion's head in filmed adaptations but, in Dickens's story, had "nothing at all peculiar about [it], except that it was very large"), momentarily turns into the face of Scrooge's partner, Jacob Marley. Who died seven years earlier, on Christmas Eve.

❋ *Marley's Ghost.* Scrooge is then visited by the apparition of his dead partner, who is bound in chains and cashboxes. This ghost also wears a bandage

wrapped under its chin to hold its jaw shut. For in Victorian England, the dead were often bound in such a manner to keep their mouths closed. Dickens himself was fitted with such a bandage after he expired on his deathbed; there's a sketch, by Sir John Everett Millais of the author wearing such a bandage, on page 77 of Michael Patrick Hearn's *The Annotated Christmas Carol*.

❁ *The Visions of the Ghost of Christmas Past*. The first Christmas Spirit, described in Dickens's story as looking like a young child *and* an old man, with "a bright clear jet of light" springing from the crown of its head, shows Scrooge key scenes from his youth. These include the lonely Christmas holidays he spent at school before his sister Fan (and *not* "Fran," as stated in various film versions; "Fanny" was the name of Dickens's favorite sister) came to take young Ebenezer home. Other Scroogian Christmas Past scenes include Scrooge's employment with the jolly Mr. Fezziwig, who knew how to celebrate Christmas; and Scrooge's engagement to and breakup with his fiancée, whose name is Belle.

❁ *The Visions of the Ghost of Christmas Present*. Described as a "jolly giant" in Dickens's original, Christmas Present shows Scrooge the poor but happy holiday being celebrated by the family of Bob Cratchit, who happens to have a sweet, lame, and very sickly son named Tiny Tim. Scrooge also witnesses the festivities at nephew Fred's Christmas party.

⚜ *Ignorance and Want.* Christmas Present lifts his robes to reveal the huddled, shivering forms of two "yellow, meagre, ragged, scowling, wolfish" Spirits. They look like a young boy and a girl, and are named Ignorance and Want.

⚜ *The Ghost of Christmas Yet-to-Come.* According to Dickens, this "Phantom . . . was shrouded in a deep black garment, which concealed its head, its face, its form, and left nothing of it visible save one outstretched hand." This specter now shows Scrooge three businessmen laughing at Ebenezer's recent death; Scrooge's own charwoman and undertaker stealing personal possessions off Scrooge's dead body and selling them to a man called Old Joe; the aftermath of the death of Tiny Tim, which leaves only "a vacant seat in the poor chimney corner, and a crutch without an owner, carefully preserved." Finally, the Ghost of Christmas Yet-to-Come shows Scrooge his own grave.

⚜ *Scrooge's Transformation.* Finding himself still alive on Christmas Day, a joyous Ebenezer calls from his bedroom window to a young boy playing in the street to buy a Christmas turkey for the Cratchits. Scrooge then attends his nephew's Christmas party, apologizes for his past behavior, and gives Bob Cratchit a raise in pay—after pretending to fire him for being late for work.

These are the key points to *A Christmas Carol*. But why did Dickens write this story in the first place? Whom did he have in mind as real-life inspirations for

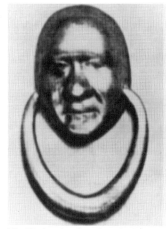

The Marley doorknocker which hung on the front door of No. 8 Craven Street in the 1840s. Presumed to be the inspiration for the ghostly image.

its fictional characters? And what impact did this *Carol* have on the way we perceive and celebrate Christmas today?

By 1843, Charles Dickens had already become a champion for social reform. One of his prime obsessions was the education of poor children. The London of Dickens's time was teeming with starving, illiterate *Kinder* of both sexes, and unless these doomed youngsters were properly educated and given the basic necessities of food and shelter, Dickens firmly believed these same children would someday rise up to tear apart the very fabric of civilization.

This pragmatic mixture of social concern and personal selfishness tells us a lot about Dickens's character. It also explains the appearance of those two ghostly infants, Ignorance and Want (a scene most filmed adaptations have chosen to ignore, by the way, with the notable exceptions of the Alastair Sim and George C. Scott versions).

Yet the *main* reason Charles Dickens created the story for which he is best known is a far more pragmatic one.

He did it for the money.

Dickens essentially tossed off *A Christmas Carol* to make a quick profit. Profits to support his growing family, which by 1843 numbered his wife, Catherine, sons Charles Culliford Boz and Walter Landor, and daughters Mary and Kate. Profits to pay back the various loans he had taken out from his London publishers, Chapman and Hall, who'd earlier published *The Pickwick Papers* and *Nicholas*

Nickleby. Profits to salt away as a hedge against his ever-present fear of poverty.

For ironically, like his father before him, Charles Dickens often teetered on the brink of financial collapse.

Dickens was also emotionally upset at the time he composed *A Christmas Carol*. Hard at work on a novel titled *Martin Chuzzlewit*, which he considered one of his most important works (and which, like most of his novels, was being serialized in a magazine), Dickens was dismayed to discover that this heartfelt effort was not selling very well. In fact, Dickens's publishers had invoked a penalty clause in the writer's contract to recoup a part of their advance.

In any event, strapped for money and unhappy with the lukewarm reception given *Chuzzlewit*, Dickens was casting about for another project when the basic idea for *A Christmas Carol* crystalized in his mind. This occurred while the author was taking a short trip to Manchester in late 1843. The occasion was a speaking engagement and fund-raiser at the Manchester Athenaeum, a charitable center of education and recreation for the working class. (Dickens shared the podium that day with noted politician Benjamin Disraeli, which gives some indication of how famous the author had already become.)

Dickens now temporarily set aside work on his "masterpiece" (*Chuzzlewit*) to churn out a popular holiday season tale, one which, he hoped, would generate some quick cash, since the author felt this new story would be perceived by his readership as the perfect present to send to their friends on Christmas. To maxi-

mize his profits, Dickens decided he'd publish it himself.

Regardless of his motivations, the author soon found himself literally obsessed with the creation of his new work. *A Christmas Carol* was written in a frenzy of activity; it took only six weeks from the moment he first set pen to paper to the day the book was published. During this period Dickens was so fixated on the themes of his story that he was literally unable to sleep; he would walk the late-night London streets laughing, crying, and talking to himself, totally caught up in the lives of his characters.

What were those themes and characters based on?

Dickens scholars agree that *A Christmas Carol* is a fascinating reflection of the immediate problems then worrying its author. For example, the theme of *Martin Chuzzlewit* was "how selfishness propagates itself, and to what a grim giant it may grow from small beginnings." Obviously, the tale of Ebenezer Scrooge was an expansion of the same theme, only this time using fantasy. And those familiar with Dickens's *Pickwick Papers* will realize that the author "professionally recycled" bits from this story as well: one *Pickwick* plot element has a surly old man being visited by goblins who show him the past and future.

But what about Scrooge?

As Dickens himself later confessed in a letter to a friend, Scrooge was a commentary on the author's own sense of guilt. Throughout his stories, Dickens had stressed that material considerations were far outweighed by the simple virtues

of the common man. These included a love of family and a strong sense of community. And Dickens wanted very much to be like the happy Cratchits, who did not let poverty destroy their happiness.

Instead, the author often felt like Scrooge. Both Scrooge *and* Dickens were obsessed with the need to make money and enjoy the benefits of wealth. Both men had unhappy childhoods. Both were pulled from school at an early age and forced to go to work.

More important than Dickens's guilt, however, is the fact that *A Christmas Carol* is ultimately a story of Ebenezer Scrooge's *redemption*. So by writing such an intensely personal examination of his own darker characteristics, it could be argued that Charles Dickens was actually trying to redeem himself through this work.

In any event, Dickens introduced other elements into *A Christmas Carol* besides his own personality.

Bob Cratchit's small terraced house, for example, was based on a similar dwelling on Bayham Street, where the Dickens family had lived when they first moved to London.

Some of the first words found in *A Christmas Carol*—"dead as a door-nail"— came to Dickens earlier that summer, when he'd dreamed of a friend being pronounced "as dead as a door-nail."

As for Tiny Tim, this character seems to be an amalgam of Dickens's own brother Frederick (who at the age of two was called "Tiny Fred"), and nephew Harry Burnett. Harry was the son of Fanny, Dickens's elder sister, and was a weak, crippled boy born in 1839.

Dickens finally completed *A Christmas Carol* after the aforementioned six weeks of work. It was now time to present it to the public—in a first edition just as luscious as its storyline.

The first-edition *Christmas Carol* was a slim hardcover book published by Chapman and Hall. Since Dickens had gone to great pains to make it *his* book (he was, after all, paying for it), he insisted that this first edition be given the finest possible packaging.

Accordingly, it was bound in red cloth, had a gilt design on the cover, and was emblazoned with gilt-edged pages. Artist John Leech provided four full-color interior etchings; four black-and-white woodcuts were also included in the book. Furthermore, this carefully designed, handsomely crafted item was a real steal, priced at the then relatively low sum of five shillings (twenty-five cents).

Consumers sat up and took notice. This edition of *A Christmas Carol* sold six thousand copies in its first *five days* of publication (sales numbers that are impressive by even today's

Fezziwig's famous party from the frontispiece by John Leech of Christmas Books, *"Cheap Editions of the Works of Charles Dickens," 1852.*

standards!), making it the most successful Christmas book of its season. And it continued to sell. By 1844, the book was already being called "a national institution."

Not bad for a piece of radical literature. After all, *A Christmas Carol* is basically an attack not only upon greed but upon those who spurn the poor and the unemployed. And in a sense, it also had a profound influence upon the very way we celebrate Christmas itself.

To understand that influence, we must first understand that in 1843 England, Christmas was not at all the "festive season" Dickens imagined for his book. Instead, it was basically a one-day holiday where presents were given to children. Period.

There were no Christmas cards or Christmas firecrackers (these came to England in, respectively, 1846 and the 1850s). No large, happy gatherings of far-flung family members reunited on Christmas day. No general spirit of benevolence and generosity. In fact, the Christmas of Charles Dickens's time was a short period of quiet rest, of reading aloud and staying at home.

But gradually, *A Christmas Carol* began to change all that. The book was so wildly popular that Dickens's story actually helped *transform* the very mythology of Christmas itself, from a rather staid religious holiday into the festive season we now know today. Which is, of course, filled with eating and drinking and gift giving to all. And, most important, with *goodwill toward men.*

That goodwill is *A Christmas Carol*'s greatest accomplishment. Charles

Dickens's "little story" nudged Christmas away from an emphasis on the particular (the family) toward an embrace of the general (all mankind). It helped transform Christmas into a *spiritual* holiday, one filled with charity, kind thoughts, and good deeds. That *one book* achieved this alchemy by mixing mysticism with reality, by contrasting the cozy comforts of home with the spine-tingling shadows of the grave, makes that accomplishment all the more remarkable.

The irony of all this is that Charles Dickens initially *lost* money on *A Christmas Carol.* He'd hoped to make at least a thousand pounds on the book (roughly four thousand dollars). But even with its impressive sales figures, *A Christmas Carol* sold only half as well as Dickens expected. By the time Chapman and Hall deducted their own expenses (needed to obtain the high-quality first edition Dickens had insisted on), the author ultimately only earned the munificent sum of 230 pounds—or, very roughly, about a thousand dollars.

Worse, a flagrantly pirated, "improved" version of *A Christmas Carol* (complete with songs!) appeared in one of London's two weekly penny newspapers shortly after the original book's release. An outraged Dickens sued and easily won his case. However, the pirates went bankrupt, and Dickens not only failed to receive damages for the loss of revenue caused by this unauthorized edition but also was stuck with court costs. These amounted to more than Dickens made from the book!

Fortunately, the popularity of *A Christmas Carol* continued to grow throughout Dickens's lifetime, so much so that its author was eventually able to

make a comfortable secondary income simply by giving public readings of the story.

Charles Dickens's first public reading of *A Christmas Carol* took place December 27, 1854. The occasion was a benefit for the newly established Birmingham and Midland Institute, one of the author's many charitable enterprises. The hall was packed with over two thousand people, who greeted the author's performance with tumultuous applause. Three days later, Dickens did another reading at a reduced price for working people.

The reception to this initial outing was so positive that other charities immediately deluged the author with requests for readings of their own. At first he refused, but the following Christmas again found Dickens on the stage. He soon discovered that traveling the provinces with his readings benefited him in a number of ways: as a solid aid for the worthwhile causes he espoused, as an outlet for his frenzied energies, and as a way to escape his increasingly unhappy marriage, which was foundering back at home.

Besides, Dickens's generosity and desire to maintain a respectable lifestyle were still keeping him in constant debt. Therefore, it was only logical that a short time after he began reading *A Christmas Carol* for charity, Charles Dickens hit on the idea of doing these performances for profit.

His friends were appalled. Dickens's contemporaries had done lectures for money, but the idea of this particularly lofty man of letters stooping to the vulgarity of the stage was quite another matter. However, Charles dismissed these objec-

tions and launched a new series of readings—beginning with *A Christmas Carol*—to public triumph.

He took his readings seriously. Originally, it had taken Dickens three hours to do *A Christmas Carol*, but he diligently pruned away at his reading copy, speeding up the narrative and tightening the dialogue. His personal copy of the book was filled with his own notated stage directions. And after he had developed this format, Dickens committed it to memory, keeping a copy on stage with him only as a fallback.

In 1865, the author brought his readings—which by now encompassed other Dickensian works—to the United States. He began in Boston with *A Christmas Carol*.

The night before the box office opened, a line formed that stretched half a mile by morning. Tickets cost two dollars apiece, but scalpers hawked them for as much as $26 each to an eager public. Many of the leading American literary figures of the day also attended that first performance.

The same phenomenon greeted Dickens in New York, where five thousand people waited throughout a cold, bitter night for a chance to buy tickets. He then performed in Philadelphia, Baltimore, and Washington, where he was invited to meet President Andrew Johnson. Exhausted, the author turned down offers to play further West, disappointing the citizens of Chicago, St. Louis, and Cincinnati.

A Christmas Carol was also the last public reading Charles Dickens ever

"The Spirit of Christmas Present" by John Tenniel, Punch, *December 30, 1893.*

gave, in 1870. Despite his failing health, the author was determined to fulfill a commitment for one final set of readings scheduled for that year. Dickens would lay stretched out speechless on a sofa during intermissions, as doctors checked his rapidly rising pulse. Somehow, though, the author would pull himself back together and return to the stage.

The last reading of the 1870 series came on March 15. As Dickens finished the final words of *A Christmas Carol*, the audience gave him a thunderous ovation, screaming that the author return for another bow. Dickens did—and with tears streaming down his cheeks announced that that particular audience had just witnessed his final performance.

Ultimately, Charles Dickens gave almost 450 public readings (not counting the ones he did for charity). *A Christmas Carol* remained the most popular of all his selections.

Then came June 9, 1870, and the world mourned the loss of a beloved figure.

Yet there's still a great deal more *Christmas Carol* story trivia Ye Author hasn't touched on. Such as:

❄ Charles Dickens was only thirty-two when he wrote *A Christmas Carol.*

❄ He made a tradition of reading it to the public every holiday season.

- Because he enjoyed its supernatural aspects so much, Dickens told people *A Christmas Carol* should be only read aloud. By candlelight. In a cold room.

- During the 1840s, *A Christmas Carol* consistently outsold the Bible!

- Scrooge's immortal line "Bah, humbug!" actually started out as "Merry Christmas, humbug!"

- Today, the original manuscript of *A Christmas Carol* is owned by and on display at the Pierpont Morgan Library in Manhattan. But Dickens's story is hardly a museum piece. In fact, every weekend in December, in the little town of Rochester, situated within County Kent, England—the same town where Dickens lived in his Gad's Hill home, a house that's now a school—the villagers dress up in nineteenth-century costumes to re-create *A Christmas Carol* all over the town. This pageant has become a much-visited English tourist attraction, and if you're ever in the vicinity, Ye Author urges you to go.

Because at Rochester, lovers of *A Christmas Carol* will find a living, breathing recreation of a modern fairy tale.

The only modern fairy tale of the Industrial Age, in fact.

One that is still the best celebration of the Christmas spirit today.

Not only as it is, but as we would *like* it to be.

TRIVIA QUESTIONS

The following questions pertain only to the *printed* version of *A Christmas Carol*, not its many film and television adaptations (we'll get to those later). And unlike the puzzlers regarding the life and work of Charles Dickens, the answers to these questions—most of them, anyway—can be found somewhere in this book.

The ones you *can't* find are in Dickens's original story. So go to the library or bookstore or borrow a copy from a friend—and read it! (Answers on page 211)

Creating "A Christmas Carol"

1. When was *A Christmas Carol* first published? By whom? Who was primarily responsible for the first edition's "look"?

2. What year saw the introduction of the first Christmas cards?

   a. 1850   b. 1846   c. 1843

3. When did Dickens first start writing *A Christmas Carol*?

4. What is Tiny Tim's favorite expression?

5. Name three real-life incidents that Dickens incorporated into *A Christmas Carol*.

6. How old was Dickens when he wrote this story?

   a. 31   b. 35   c. 42   d. 32   e. 34

7. Who illustrated the first edition? How much did that book cost?

8. What is the biggest change that *A Christmas Carol* has made on the Christmas season itself?

9. Where can the original manuscript of *A Christmas Carol* be seen today?

10. Everyone knows that Scrooge's favorite exclamation is "Bah, humbug!" But what was Dickens's *original* version of this line?

11. Name two prior works that Dickens cannibalized to reuse for *A Christmas Carol.*

12. In what English town did Dickens have his Gad's Hill house?

13. Which book (in England) did *A Christmas Carol* consistently outsell during the 1840s?

14. How many copies of its first edition did *A Christmas Carol* sell immediately after its release? In how many days?

    a. 6,000 copies—seven days   b. 5,000 copies—six days   c. 6,000 copies—five days

15. What famous English politician once shared a public speaking engagement with Charles Dickens?

16. What unusual behavior did Dickens exhibit during the writing of *A Christmas Carol?*

17. When did Dickens finalize the idea for *A Christmas Carol?* On what occasion?

18. Give two reasons why Charles Dickens wrote *A Christmas Carol.*

19. Name Ebenezer Scrooge's dead partner. For those of you who've actually *read* the story—what is this partner's ghostly punishment? What does he do to convince Scrooge that he's really dead?

20. What is Ebenezer Scrooge's profession?

21. When was the first public reading of *A Christmas Carol* performed by Charles Dickens? The last?

22. Approximately how many public readings did Dickens give in his lifetime?

23. How much did a ticket cost to attend the author's first public reading of *A Christmas Carol* in America? Where was that reading held? When?

24. How long did it take Dickens to originally read the unedited version of his tale?

25. What "addition" did the pirated version of *A Christmas Carol*—the one against which Dickens successfully sued—add to the author's story?

CHAPTER THREE
THE BEST VERSION

A CHRISTMAS CAROL (AKA *SCROOGE*) (GREAT BRITAIN, 1951) RATING: ★★★★

he rest of this book will concentrate on the many different ways *A Christmas Carol* has been adapted for the big screen and small, for children's cartoons, or for home video. And Ye Author can think of no better way to begin this examination than with a separate chapter devoted to the greatest version of all.

But, as the following review makes clear, this classic filmed version of *Carol* wasn't exactly hailed as masterpiece during its first appearance.

"This British import, which United Artists is distributing in the States, hasn't enough entertainment merit to rate it anything but slim chances. It's a grim thing that will give tender-aged kiddies viewing it the screaming-meemies, and adults will find it long, dull, and greatly overdone. There's certainly no Yuletide cheer to be found in this latest interpretation of Charles Dickens's Christmas classic."

And there's certainly no better example of a critic shooting himself in the foot than this!

This quote was excerpted from the November 14, 1951, issue of *Variety*. Written over forty years ago by a regular reviewer who by-lined himself "Brog.," this review immediately raises a number of questions:

Was "Brog." in a bad mood that day?

Hungry?

Asleep?

Dead?

For one fact throws his off-the-mark opinions into a retrospectively hilarious light.

Not only does the 1951 *Christmas Carol* contain *none* of the flaws mentioned in "Brog.'s" review, this motion picture is now generally accepted as the best *Carol* ever filmed!

Made at England's Nettlefold Studios by Renown Film Productions Ltd., a small British company headed by George Minter (a former English journalist turned producer/distributor, who would again tackle Dickens in a 1952 adaptation of *The*

Scrooge (Alastair Sim) takes his meager dinner before meeting Marley's Ghost in the superior 1951 version of A Christmas Carol.

Pickwick Papers), the 1951 *Christmas Carol* has gained a tremendous stature and respectability since its negative *Variety* review. In fact, next to *It's a Wonderful Life*, the "Alastair Sim *Carol*" (as it's commonly called) is far and away the most popular Yuletide film of the season, televised annually on many stations in the United States.

Paradoxically, this is also quite a *somber Christmas Carol* (which should put to rest the lie that audiences only want "upbeat" entertainment). It doesn't avoid the darker elements of Dickens's parable by drowning its story in syrupy Hollywood sentiment; on the contrary, the overall "look" of the 1951 *Carol* is dark, forbidding, and at times quite eerie, perfectly reflecting the ghost story at its core. And Dickens's social concerns aren't forgotten, either. Images of poverty and want repeatedly occur throughout the film—the carolers the 1951 Scrooge encounters, for example, are a trio of bedraggled beggar children singing for alms, forced to ply their pitiful trade on a desolate, snow-swept street.

But what is it—what is it *exactly*—that makes this version so superior to the rest?

Could it be director Brian Desmond-Hurst's evocative recreation of nineteenth-century London? Ralph Brinton's scrupulous production design? Noel Langley's faithful, novelistic script, which reveals a density of character and incident not found in most other versions of *Carol*?

Actually, there are many reasons. Like any classic motion picture, the 1951

Carol is compellingly directed, well photographed, and sensitively acted. Yet these qualities only begin to explain why this version outshines its competition; the 1951 *Carol* has an abundance of riches almost impossible to catalog in one short chapter of a book.

But Ye Author will try.

Perhaps the best place to start is with its cast. The 1951 *Carol* teems with excellent performances by talented actors, who are perfectly cast down to the smallest part. Standouts include Mervyn Johns as the gentle Bob Cratchit; Glyn Dearman as an endearing Tiny Tim; comical Kathleen Harrison as Scrooge's housekeeper; Michael Hordern as the supernaturally tormented Jacob Marley (whose lines "I am doomed to wander without rest or peace. Incessant torture and remorse!" are genuinely moving); and dry, droll Ernest Thesiger (Dr. Praetorius from *The Bride of Frankenstein*) as a larcenous undertaker. Cult movie fans will also enjoy a brief performance by the actor who plays young Marley; this is Patrick Macnee, the same thespian who'd later rocket to worldwide fame as debonair secret agent John Steed, on the wild mid-sixties television show *The Avengers*.

Yet one performer towers above all others in this motion picture. Indeed, he's the emotional glue that holds the entire production together.

His name is Alastair Sim.

Born October 9, 1900, in Edinburgh, Scotland, Sim's fame has risen above being merely praised as the best performer to ever portray Ebenezer Scrooge—for most filmgoers, Sim *is* Ebenezer Scrooge! An eccentric character actor with sad eyes and inimitable diction, Sim was actually a teacher of phonetics and elocution before entering show business at the age of thirty. His first acting appearance was on the London stage. A few years later, Sim's popular performance as the Mad Hatter in a successful English stage version of *Alice in Wonderland* caught the eye of British film producers, and the Scottish actor began his cinematic career in 1935.

Alastair Sim's affinity for quirky dramas and sly comedies quickly made him a film industry favorite. He appeared in many memorable pictures—including *Green for Danger* (1946), *The Belles of St. Trinian's* (1954), and *The Ruling Class* (1972)—before his last role in *Escape From the Dark* (1976). He died the same year, after four decades of consistently impressive work.

Throughout his fruitful career, Sim was routinely praised for investing his characters with droll wit and wonderful expressiveness. Nowhere are these qualities more evident than in *A Christmas Carol*; Sim's Scrooge is a three-dimensional, truly *alive* creation, one relying on much more than just sentimental shadings.

For instance, unlike many other Ebenezers (who are rou-

Marley's Ghost (Michael Hordern) visits a terrified Ebenezer Scrooge.

tinely caricatured as stereotyped misers), Sim's is the only Scrooge who seems like a *businessman*. His character exudes the distraction of a man consumed by daily commerce, one whose sense of arrogant self-superiority conveys the philosophy that the world is not only a hard and cruel place, but that only the strong will survive in that place.

The best example of this arrogance occurs in a marvelous scene where the young Scrooge and Marley have deftly maneuvered themselves into gaining possession of the company run by their embezzling employer, Mr. Jorkins (Jack Warner). Sim doesn't say a word during this sequence. He merely sits there, hands crossed in lap, a faint smile on his lips. But the smug triumph projected by that smile speaks volumes about Scrooge's ruthlessness.

However, Sim can just as easily project tenderness. The scene in which Ebenezer relives the loneliness of his schoolboy days (where his sister Fran explains that their father always blamed Scrooge for the death of their mother, who died giving Ebenezer birth, a theme that would be expanded more than thirty years later in the George C. Scott *Christmas Carol*) is genuinely poignant. It's exactly sequences like these—as well as the film's insistence on giving us such a long, detailed look at Scrooge's past—that give Sim the opportunity to so satisfyingly flesh out Ebenzer's complex personality.

Yet these extra dimensions shouldn't suggest that the 1951 *Carol* ignores Scrooge's more familiar mannerisms. For example, when Sim barks out "Bah, hum-

Scrooge (Alastair Sim) and the Spirit of the Present (Francis De Wolff) at the home of Bob Cratchit (Mervyn Johns, foreground).

bug!" those words have real bite. And director Brian Desmond-Hurst cleverly suggests Scrooge's miserliness through a number of subtle *visual* clues: Sim wears a worn, dirty coat with faintly smudged lapels; Scrooge's thick bed curtains have long, ragged rips in them.

So part of the greatness of the 1951 *Carol* is a Scrooge who's both human *and* nasty. Here's a man who can be easily heartbroken by the death of his former sweetheart, or callously put off a visit to his dying partner, just so he can finish a day's work. Sim's isn't a Scrooge easily reformed, either. As Ebenezer tells the Ghost of Christmas Present (Francis De Wolff), "I am too old to change!"

Yet change he does. Alastair Sim caps off this terrific performance by completely throwing over the darker aspects of his personality during the justifiably famous "Christmas morning" scene. And no one's been better at conveying the relief, ecstasy, and sheer love of life Ebenezer celebrates after surviving his encounter with the three Christmas Ghosts. To watch the exhilarated capering of this totally reformed rascal—Sim even stands on his head!—is to witness one of the most joyous scenes of spiritual conversion ever put on the screen.

Of course, Alastair Sim's incredible performance didn't occur in a vacuum.

The director of *A Christmas Carol* was Brian Desmond-Hurst. An Irishman born February 12, 1900, in Castle Reagh, he expatriated to Hollywood in 1925 and served as an assistant to legendary Western filmmaker John Ford before traveling on to England to direct his own films. This profession started in 1934. Desmond-

Hurst then enjoyed a thirty-year career and worked in a variety of genres—adventures, comedies, and dramas. Some of his better efforts are the British aerial warfare story *Dangerous Moonlight* (1941); the gripping *Simba* (1955), about a vicious uprising staged by the revolutionary African Mau-Maus; and an eloquent adaptation of J. M. Synge's classic Irish satire *The Playboy of the Western World* (1962).

But it's *A Christmas Carol* that remains the crown jewel in Desmond-Hurst's career. There's a mystical, almost dreamlike atmosphere to this film, one that immediately draws us into the plot and never lets go. Mood is everything here—and what a mood it is! Deep shadows, Richard Addinsell's ominous musical score, a frightening Ghost of Christmas Yet-to-Come, a graveyard scene that seems like something straight out of a Hammer film . . . at times, this *Christmas Carol* almost plays like a horror movie.

Yet not all is doom and gloom. Desmond-Hurst also injects memorable moments of sweetness (the close-up of Tiny Tim proclaiming "God bless us, every one!"), visual shorthand (Scrooge's time-traveling is suggested by an hourglass hurtling down a rocky tunnel aflurry with falling snowflakes), pathos (Cratchit weeping over the death of Tim), and gaiety (that marvelous little jig the reformed Scrooge dances on Christmas morning). Plus this director mounts an astonishingly vivid recreation of nineteenth-century Victorian England.

To this end, Desmond-Hurst was ably assisted by the gritty, occasionally sinister black-and-white cinematography of C. Pennington-Richards, as well as by the haunting art direction of Ralph Hinton. The London of the 1951 *Carol* is a teeming, vivid place crammed with city streets, public houses, banks, inns, offices, and homes. Furthermore, the convincing production design serves a symbolic purpose—has there ever been a gloomier visual metaphor for a miser's spiritual poverty than the gloomy bedchamber inhabited by this Ebenezer Scrooge?

So come next Christmas, gather the family around that electronic fire known as the television set and savor the 1951 *Christmas Carol* once again. You'll see a classic. Drenched in atmosphere. Faithful to its source material. Meticulously acted, designed, and directed. A superb motion picture which critic Leonard Maltin has rightly described as being "too good to be only enjoyed at Christmas time."

It concludes with these famous lines:

"Scrooge was better than his word. He became as good a friend, as good a master, and as good a man as the good old city ever knew, or any other good old city, town, or borough in the good old world. And to Tiny Tim, who lived and got better again, he became a second father. And it was always said that he knew how to keep Christmas well, if any man possessed the

The Cratchit family pour out the gin punch as Scrooge and the Ghost of Christmas Present look on.

knowledge. May that be truly said of us, and all of us.
"And so, as Tiny Tim observed—
"God bless us, everyone."

And God bless Alastair Sim!

TRIVIA QUESTIONS

There are more trivia questions in this chapter than in any other section of the book. But that's only fitting, since we've just examined the best version of *A Christmas Carol*!

However, from this point onward, the only way you'll be able to answer *every* trivia question is to actually *view* the various adaptations this book discusses. In other words, for maximum enjoyment, you should watch the various video, television, or film versions first. *Then* answer the questions! (Answers are listed on page 213)

A Christmas Carol (aka *Scrooge*)

1. How old was Alastair Sim before he turned to acting? What was his former profession?

2. Which behind-the-scenes person worked on both the 1951 version and another,

later Carol? What year did he labor on this second adaptation and what was his function on each?

3. This one's easy: Name the original English title of the 1951 Christmas Carol.

4. The first shot of the 1951 Carol shows a bookshelf with a row of novels on it. A hand then reaches into frame and withdraws a volume labeled A Christmas Carol. Name the titles of two other books which can be seen on the bookshelf.

5. Two actors who appear in the 1951 version of the film went on to star in another adaptation of the same story—but the second time, audiences never saw their faces! Name these actors and the parts they played, as well as the title of this later adaptation.

6. The music which runs over the opening credits of the 1951 *Carol* is a familiar Christmas song. Name it. Now name another (film) version of *A Christmas Carol* which uses the same song over *its* opening credits.

7. Just before the 1951 film's narration begins, we see a close-up of a page from Charles Dickens's original story. What words do we see on this page?

8. Where does the 1951 version's first scene take place?

9. What is the first thing that Bob Cratchit does when Ebenezer arrives at the offices of Scrooge & Marley?

10. Give the time Scrooge arrives at his office.

Scrooge is shown his childhood by the Spirit of Christmas Past (Michael Dolan).

Goodtimes Home Video box art: A Christmas Carol *(1951).*

11. What is Scrooge's reply to the two gentlemen who come to his office seeking charity for the poor, after being told by them that the poor would rather die than go to the poorhouse?

12. When we first meet her, what is Mrs. Cratchit shopping for?

13. While Scrooge is eating his dinner at the tavern, what does he ask a waiter for? Why doesn't he get it?

14. What does Scrooge hear as he's going up the staircase in his house?

15. At what time does Marley's Ghost appear?

16. We know from a line earlier in the film that when *A Christmas Carol* begins, Jacob Marley has been dead exactly seven years. But how many years did Scrooge and Marley *work* together?

17. When Scrooge asks Marley's Ghost what he wants of him, what does the latter reply?

18. *A Christmas Carol* is filled with classic bits of dialogue that show up in virtually every version of the story. One such line comes when Marley's Ghost asks Scrooge why the miser doesn't believe in him. Quote the classic reply Scrooge makes to Marley's Ghost. (HINT: It has something to do with food.)

19. When Marley's Ghost takes him to a window and makes him look out on the street, what does Scrooge see?

20. At what time does the Ghost of Christmas Past arrive?

21. Why is Scrooge afraid to go out the window with the Ghost of Christmas Past?

22. Another classic *Christmas Carol* scene occurs when the Ghost of Christmas Past takes Scrooge back to his days as a schoolboy and the young Ebenezer is visited by his kindly sister. This sister tells Scrooge that she's come to take him home for the holidays. What is the sister's name? And what happens during this scene (in the 1951 *Carol*) that occurs in no other filmed version of the story? Finally, what's the name of the traditional ballad heard playing in the background of this scene?

23. What was the young Scrooge's job with his old employer, Fezziwig?

24. Name young Scrooge's fiancée.

25. Fezziwig is usually given no first name in any other version of the story. But in this 1951 adaptation, you *do* get to see the first *initial* of Fezziwig's name. What is it? Where do you see it?

26. What then-unknown but now-famous character actor plays the part of the young Jacob Marley? Name the hit series this English actor later starred in during the sixties, plus the name of the character he played.

27. Near the end of the Christmas Past sequence, we get a rare chance to find out not only what kind of business Fezziwig was involved with, but also the year he established it. Can you describe Fezziwig's business and the year it began?

28. The young Marley and Scrooge both end up working for Mr. Jorkin before they ultimately buy out his business. What's the name of Jorkin's company?

29. What must Scrooge first do before he can travel with the Ghost of Christmas Present?

30. How does Bob Cratchit carry Tiny Tim home from church?

31. What kind of punch do the Cratchit family have for Christmas dinner? A punch that both the adults and children enjoy?

32. When the Ghost of Christmas Present lifts its robes to show a horrified Scrooge the skeletal spirits of Ignorance and Want, which Spirit does Christmas Present warn Ebenezer to beware most of all?

33. What does the Ghost of Christmas Yet-to-Come look like in this version? Do you ever see its face? Does it talk?

34. Where do Scrooge's charwoman, laundress, and undertaker meet to sell Ebenezer's things after he's dead? What objects does the undertaker sell?

35. What does Scrooge ask the Ghost of Christmas Yet-to-Come just before Ebenezer looks at his own tombstone?

36. What is the date of Scrooge's death, according to what's chiseled on that tombstone?

37. When the reformed Scrooge is in his bedroom on Christmas morning, there's a minor (and anachronistic) technical error that occurs *twice* during the scene where Sim is talking with his charwoman. Most people never catch this blooper, but once you do, you'll never be able to *not* see it again. What is this error? (HINT: It involves a mirror).

38. According to this version of the story, what is the address of Bob Cratchit's house?

39. When Cratchit returns to work the day after Christmas and the reformed Scrooge raises his salary, what does Ebenezer then order the astonished Bob to rush out and buy before Cratchit "dots another 'i'"?

40. Some versions of *A Christmas Carol* end with Tiny Tim saying "God bless us, every one!" But although Tiny Tim gets the last word in this adaptation too, he *doesn't* say "God bless us, every one"! What *are* Tiny Tim's last words in the 1951 *Carol*?

CHAPTER FOUR
RECOMMENDED FILM VERSIONS

O f all the feature-length film versions of *A Christmas Carol*, only three have stood the test of time. One, of course, is the Alastair Sim version. The other two were made in 1935 and 1938.

These latter two films are somewhat dissimilar in their adaptive approach to *A Christmas Carol*, and strikingly different in terms of tone. Which only goes to prove that one of the enduring strengths of Dickens's story is its flexibility. Like a good Shakespearean play, *A Christmas Carol*'s themes are so universal that the trappings surrounding those themes—locale, time-period, etc.—are capable of being radically altered without changing the narrative's central concerns. The story's setting, for example; this could easily be switched from Victorian London to a small town in Depression-era America, as occurs in *An American Christmas Carol*. Or the tale's time-frame—the mid-nineteenth century—could be pushed forward centuries into the future (*A Jetsons Christmas Carol*).

But back to the 1935 and 1938 *Carols*, which are minor classics in their own right. Even if they don't quite achieve the Olympian heights scaled by the Sim version.

The 1935 version is British and remains largely unseen in this country.

The 1938 film is American and is probably more popular than the 1951 film version. (Not better, you understand, just more *popular*).

Both are available on videotape.

SCROOGE (AKA *A CHRISTMAS CAROL*) (GREAT BRITAIN, 1935) RATING: ★★★

Although originally released in its native England by Paramount Pictures, this early, black-and-white British *Carol* is not a well-known film. Cable television and videocassettes are slowly beginning to change its obscure status, however; the 1935 *Scrooge* now pops up around Christmastime, and it can also be found on budget-minded video labels like *Goodtimes* and *Viking Video Classics*.

Perhaps the simplest phrase that sums up this 1935 production is

What Happened When Scrooge Saw Marley's Face on the Knocker . . . and the Clock Struck Twelve!

"SCROOGE"

based on
"A CHRISTMAS CAROL"
by
CHARLES DICKENS
A Paramount Release with
SIR SEYMOUR HICKS
DONALD CALTHROP
Directed by Henry Edwards
A Julius Hagen-Twickenham Production
T H E A T R E

The lobby card for Scrooge.

"good, but not great." On the plus side are *Scrooge*'s screenplay and direction. Much of the film's dialogue is plucked directly from the original story, and there's an earnest attempt by director Henry Edwards to preserve an impressive period atmosphere–among the film's greatest strengths–without bogging down the pace. At times it seems you're peering through a window at a dim, smoky moment in 1843; it's as if your television set had turned into a time machine.

Also impressive are the film's special effects and performances. The Ghost of Christmas Past, for instance, is displayed as an eerie, glowing, vaguely humanoid mass of light. And British actor Donald Calthrop is an excellent Bob Cratchit. Whether patiently maintaining his temper under the withering abuse heaped upon him by Scrooge, or lovingly celebrating Christmas with his family, Calthrop's Cratchit is never less than believable. Which is not an easy thing: many lesser productions have flattened out Cratchit's character to the thickness of a cardboard saint (even Mervyn Johns, in his otherwise fine 1951 Cratchit characterization, relied a bit too much on eccentric meekness).

But the greatest achievement of the 1935 version has to be the Ebenezer Scrooge of Sir Seymour Hicks.

Born in 1871, Hicks was an English actor-writer-producer who primarily appeared on the British stage. His specialty was knockabout farces; he was also well known for the many different times he played Scrooge on the English stage, beginning in 1901. Hicks further, but only occasionally, appeared in both silent and talk-

A publicity still for Scrooge *distributed to newspapers as a stereo mat.*

ing motion pictures. The author of two autobiographies (*Between Ourselves*, 1930, and *Me and My Missus*, 1939), Hicks was eventually awarded a knighthood for his artistic accomplishments (hence the "Sir"). He died in 1949.

Interestingly, Sir Seymour had already starred in a *silent* film version of *A Christmas Carol* (in 1913) before appearing in the 1935 edition. He also helped *write* both of these pictures. Hicks penned the 1913 version's screenplay by himself; he then cowrote the 1935 script with H. Fowler Mear.

As for his acting, by the time he made this version, Hicks had Scrooge down cold. His 1935 Ebenezer is a small, sour, disheveled old moneylender, whose scornful eyes and outthrust lower lip fairly drip with contempt for humanity. And he's especially good at portraying Scrooge's spiritual metamorphosis. Hicks begins the picture by gleefully chortling, "Every fool who goes around saying 'Merry Christmas' should be boiled with his own pudding and buried with a stake of holly through his heart." He ends the film clearly humbled, thoroughly chastened by his supernatural experiences.

In fact, Hicks's final transformation is not only dramatic, but refreshingly *human*. He leaves you with the feeling that Ebenezer's conversion is due in large part to the fact that he's been scared half out of his wits; here's one Scrooge who is extraordinarily grateful *just to be alive!*

Besides its unusually fine performances, the 1935 version also features an emotionally disturbing scene not found in most other cinematic versions of *Carol*

(although it does appear in Dickens's original story). This is the sequence where the Ghost of Christmas Past forces Ebenezer to watch a joyful Christmas being celebrated by the family of his ex-fiancée, Belle, who, after leaving Scrooge, married a loving husband, reared many beautiful children, and enjoyed a blissfully happy life.

This glimpse at "what might have been" adds an unusual moment of poignancy to the 1935 *Scrooge*. And it's not an easy moment to watch. For Scrooge, it's only a painful vision of loss; for the audience, it's the cruelest moment in the film.

Scrooge further boasts some extraordinary visual elements. The film's cramped, claustrophobic sets make us feel as if we've actually been catapulted back into Victorian England. And the dark, near-expressionistic cinematography by Sydney Blythe and William Luff is notable as well.

Unfortunately, some video versions of this motion picture (like the *Viking Video Classics* cassette) feature such poor, high-contrast prints that, half the time, you can't see what's going on (viewers should seek out the LP-speed *Goodtimes* cassette of *Scrooge*, which has the best picture quality). Worse, all video versions cut down the film's already short seventy-eight-minute running time to a mere sixty minutes!

Still, the major weaknesses of *Scrooge* are primarily due to technical deficits in the film itself; this movie suffers from poor lighting and rather sloppy sound recording. But since British film production methods in the mid-1930s had

not yet caught up to the high Hollywood standards of this period, these deficits are understandable . . . if not completely forgivable.

For all that, the 1935 film is still a fine addition to the ranks of celluloid versions of *A Christmas Carol*. It's a well-acted, pungently atmospheric effort.

A CHRISTMAS CAROL (USA, 1938) RATING: ★★★

Lobby card for the 1938 MGM version of A Christmas Carol.

In 1938, *A Christmas Carol* was finally adapted as a major Hollywood picture by Metro-Goldwyn-Mayer.

However, before this film was "in the can," it was easy to assume that MGM would give their version the same royal treatment it lavished upon its other pictures. And in many respects, it did.

With one crucial exception.

Money.

"The 1938 *Christmas Carol* was definitely a B picture," actress June Lockhart told the *Hollywood Reporter* in November 1988. "In those days [the major studios] took a big hit and block-booked it with a [lower budgeted film], which *A Christmas Carol* was definitely considered. In fact, MGM looked on it as a disposable project, as secondary filler. And since television hadn't come along yet, none of us had a clue that it would eventually be shown [on TV] every year."

Marley's Ghost MGM style: Leo G. Carroll (left) with Reginald Owen.

June Lockhart made her professional film debut, at the age of twelve, in MGM's *Christmas Carol.* Born June 25, 1925, in New York, she first began acting on stage when she was eight years old. Lockhart later became well known for her roles as the kindly mothers of both the old *Lost in Space* and *Lassie* TV shows (she also appeared in a Lassie *film, Son of Lassie,* in 1945). In MGM's *Christmas Carol,* Lockhart portrayed Belinda Cratchit, the screen daughter to her *real-life parents,* Gene and Kathleen Lockhart, who played Bob Cratchit and his wife (a nice in-joke!).

But enough of the Cratchits—what about Scrooge? Everyone knows that his is the pivotal role in the story. And even if MGM was not going to give its version of *A Christmas Carol* the A treatment, studio head Louis B. Mayer must have realized that casting the proper actor for Scrooge was crucial to his film's success.

Actually, Mayer had already made up his mind as to who was to play Scrooge . . . but the actor under consideration never got the part. This was Lionel Barrymore.

Barrymore's participation in the project began ordinarily enough. In 1938, he'd signed a contract to portray Scrooge, and his casting seemed a logical choice. The reason? Because the genial, avuncular actor had read *A Christmas Carol* on a nationally broadcast radio program every Christmas morning, once a year, since 1933.

This annual show was immensely popular. Indeed, to most Americans captivated by radio's then all-pervasive spell, Barrymore *was* Scrooge.

However, an attack of bad health (lameness in Barrymore's legs) caused the actor's doctor to urge Barrymore to delay filming MGM's *Carol* for at least two months. Since Barrymore was already so fondly associated with the part of Scrooge, MGM was more than willing to put off filming its version for a full year and release it in the Christmas season of 1939. This, Mayer hoped, would give the actor ample time to convalesce.

But Barrymore would have none of it. According to promotional materials distributed by MGM at the time of the 1938 *Christmas Carol*'s release, Barrymore felt that waiting another year was simply not an option. Concerned by growing jitters over the looming war in Europe, the actor supposedly told MGM, "If ever the world needed Dickens's message of peace on earth and good will toward men, that time is today."

Whether one actually believes this statement or simply views it as publicity fluff, at least one part of Barrymore's involvement with the 1938 *Christmas Carol* is a proven fact—it was he who suggested that British actor Reginald Owen step in as Scrooge.

"My friend Reginald Owen is a great actor, and I can think of nobody who could play the part [of Scrooge] as well," Barrymore was quoted as saying in MGM's *Christmas Carol* pressbook. "In addition, he is an Englishman, and I can only see an Englishman playing Dickens."

Ebenezer Scrooge meets a jolly ghost of Christmas Present (Lionel Braham).

Reginald Owen was born in 1887 and died in 1972. A native of Hartfordshire, England, he first studied for a theatrical career in Sir Herbert Tree's Academy of Dramatic Arts. After great success on the English stage he came to America to perform in play called *The Swan.* Owen then sequed into film work, appearing in a number of silent pictures before making *The Letter,* his first talkie, in 1929. He later embarked upon a long and fruitful American film career as a noted character actor, appearing in literally dozens of pictures. Among Owen's better-known works are *Queen Christina* (1933), *Of Human Bondage* (1934), *A Tale of Two Cities* (1935), *Mrs. Miniver* (1942), and *Mary Poppins* (1964).

With the casting of Scrooge, MGM still had a problem with Owen—the actor was too young for the part. Although he was fifty-one years old in 1938, Owen's tall, curly-haired good looks made him appear a full decade younger. Since this youthful handsomeness was not exactly the embodiment of a bitter old miser, it was decided that Owen would have to undergo an elaborate makeup process to age him twenty years.

Owen's makeup consisted of adding a bald cap, wrinkles, and bushy eyebrows to an otherwise youngish-looking actor. This was a process that took a full two hours a day to complete, a process supervised by the great Jack Dawn.

Dawn (along with oldest son Bob) was one of movie makeup's true pioneers. Born in Covington, Kentucky, in 1889, Dawn was fascinated by the art of sculpting and eventually drifted into Hollywood. He first became director of makeup at Fox Studios, then moved on to a similar position at Twentieth Century Pictures. Dawn later relocated to Metro-Goldwyn-Mayer, where he succeeded Cecil Holland as MGM's director of makeup.

During his twenty-five year career at MGM Jack Dawn created scores of impressive character makeups. Many remain outstanding today. While most viewers probably know Dawn best from his work on *The Wizard of Oz* (Jack found transforming Ray Bolger into the Scarecrow to be his most difficult assignment), Dawn also changed dozens of Caucasian actors into Chinese peasants for *The Good Earth*, turned Charles Boyer into Napoleon for *Conquest*, and withered a young Sam Jaffe into *Lost Horizon*'s ageless Grand Lama (all 1937).

As for *A Christmas Carol*, Dawn discovered that the blueprint for Owen's makeup had already been laid out for him. Charles Dickens had always gone to great pains to describe his characters in minute detail; therefore, Dawn based his Reginald Owen/Ebenezer Scrooge makeup on a close study of Dickens's own descriptions of Scrooge, as well as on the original *Carol* illustrations drawn by John Leech.

Now that their actor and makeup were securely in place, MGM next chose Edwin L. Marin (whose hobby of haunting auction houses and antique shops resulted in many of Marin's own possessions being used as props in the 1938 film) to direct *A Christmas Carol*.

Marin was born in 1899 in Jersey City, New Jersey. Beginning his film career as an assistant cameraman, Marin became a director in 1931, one who

A posed publicity shot depicting a fictional encounter between Tiny Tim (Terry Kilburn) and Ebenezer Scrooge.

worked on such "poverty-row" productions as *The Death Kiss* (1933) before moving up to employment at the major studios. Marin then directed films for Universal Pictures (*Invisible Agent*, 1942), RKO (*Johnny Angel*, 1945), Twentieth Century Fox (*Fighting Man of the Plains*, 1949) and Warner Brothers (*Sugarfoot*, 1950). He died in 1951.

Most of Marin's career, however, was spent at MGM. And as a traditional-minded director who seemed drawn to crime films, melodramas, and period pieces, Marin was careful to assure that his version of *A Christmas Carol* would reflect a personal concern for historical accuracy.

To this end Marin had the MGM technicians construct a full-scale reproduction of London's famed Threadneedle Street, circa 1840, to be used as one of his main sets. Marin also utilized the resources of the MGM research department, which dug up many obscure facts concerning daily life in mid-nineteenth-century London.

One was that merchants usually placed groceries in cornucopia-shaped rolls of wrapping paper. (There were no paper bags in 1843.)

The ominous Spirit of Christmas Future (D'Arcy Corrigan, right*) shows a terrified Scrooge his own dead body in this chilling moment from the 1938 film version.*

Another was the fact that it was Prince Albert who introduced Christmas trees into England. A member of the German aristocracy who'd married into British royalty, Albert was already familiar with Christmas trees, since they were very popular in his Teutonic homeland, and was surprised to discover that the English had not yet been won over to what the Prince considered a charming Germanic custom.

So, in 1840, Albert took the lead by installing the first Christmas tree in London, which he had set up inside Windsor Castle.

In any event, Marin's insistence on period authenticity also extended to food. The director wanted, and got, a real plum pudding, made in the traditional Olde English style, for the scene where the Cratchits sit down to their Christmas dinner.

This insistence led to one of the most nauseating (literally!) behind-the-scenes stories associated with the MGM *Carol*.

Marin had decided that one shot during the Cratchit dinner scene required that the plum pudding be set on fire. Yet now the director had a problem. Not because the pudding wouldn't burn—it had been liberally doused with brandy, as was the British custom, and brandy is nothing if not flammable—but because the resulting blue flame would not register on black-and-white film.

MGM's Cratchit clan: Gene Lockhart as Bob Cratchit and Terry Kilburn as Tiny Tim, surrounded by (from left) Lynne Carver, Kathleen Lockhart, Muriel Kearney, June Lockhart, and Bill Martin (hidden).

Marin's solution was to coat the entire pudding with a thick layer of salt. This produced a *yellow* flame, and allowed the fire to be photographed. The burning salt also meant that the performers would have to deliver their most convincing piece of acting. Because the Cratchit family now had to actually *eat* this heavily salted dessert, over and over again, for many different takes.

"I got horribly sick that day," recalled June Lockhart. "We were supposed to be acting so festive—but I could barely hold my head up long enough to ask the

propman, 'Could you please set this bowl of turnips in front of somebody else?' "

Despite these gastrointestinal tribulations, MGM's *Christmas Carol* finally finished filming in time for a 1938 holiday season release. In order to promote the picture, a special "Coming Attractions" short (known in the film industry as a "trailer") was shot and shipped to theaters nationwide before the picture itself was released.

This special promotional featurette was titled *A Fireside Chat with Lionel Barrymore*. It was directed by Edwin Marin. In it, Barrymore alerted audiences to the fact that a new version of *A Christmas Carol* was headed toward their local movie palaces. Barrymore also informed viewers that he himself would not be playing Scrooge. Instead, the actor took this opportunity to introduce Reginald Owen in the part.

So in a sense, it could be argued that despite a number of mishaps and delays, Lionel Barrymore finally *did* appear in *A Christmas Carol*. Or at least in the film's publicity.

But what of the picture itself? Well, in terms of overall artistic merit, Ye Author believes that the 1938 version is only the *third-best* live-action *Christmas Carol*, after the Alastair Sim adaptation and the George C. Scott one.

Which is not to say the MGM *Carol* is without its own delights. One highlight is a thoroughly charming Tiny Tim, portrayed by the then eleven-year-old Terry Kilburn. An English child actor, Kilburn found early success in such classics as the 1939 *Goodbye, Mr. Chips* (in which he portrayed boys from four different generations of the same family). Unfortunately a waning film career then led to appearances in B movies like *Fiend Without a Face* (1958). This decline prompted Kilburn to abandon filmmaking altogether and accept a position as artistic director of the Meadowbrook Theater in Rochester, Michigan.

Furthermore, and unlike the oppressive 1935 version–which gave full rein to the darker side of Dickens's ghostly fable–the MGM *Carol* resembles a festively wrapped Christmas present. Marin's London is cheerfully bright, quaint, and sparkling, scrubbed clean of any allusions to poverty or squalor. This upbeat environment echoes the film's presentation of Scrooge, who, although suitably crusty early on, is a relatively *attractive* figure, one so eager for conversion that he turns humanitarian before the picture is two-thirds over! Quite a change from Sir Seymour Hicks's portrayal, who played Scrooge as a stubbornly unrepentant, almost gnomish man.

Ultimately, however, MGM's emphasis on the positive was a shrewd move. The 1938 *Carol* remains a beloved holiday perennial, seen on dozens of local television stations every Christmas Eve. And as Ye Author stated elsewhere in this chapter, *this* is the *Christmas Carol* most viewers carry in their memories.

Perhaps the simplest way to sum up the 1938 *Carol* is "relentlessly cheerful." MGM's atmosphere of infectious gaiety reaches its peak near the film's end, in a scene guaranteed to open every tear duct in the house.

An expressionistic shot from the MGM film. Reginald Owen as Scrooge meets the ominous Spirit of Christmas Future (D'Arcy Corrigan).

For here occurs that moment wherein a reformed, gift-laden Scrooge bursts into the Cratchit home on Christmas morning.

"Everything for everybody!" Owen joyfully declares.

A sentiment perfectly suited to MGM's exuberant (and traditional) approach to Dickens's holiday classic.

TRIVIA QUESTIONS

(Answers on page 216.)

Scrooge (aka *A Christmas Carol*) (1935)

1. Name the well-known Christmas song that runs over the opening credits of this version.

2. Before the film proper begins, there's a written prologue which reproduces—word for word—the same two sentences that Dickens himself used as the prologue for his original story. Can you quote these two sentences?

3. How many children does Bob Cratchit have in this version?

4. Why does Scrooge's nephew Fred say he got married?

5. During a lavish banquet scene shown early in the film, who is the important

A repentant Scrooge is shown his own grave by the Spirit of Christmas Future.

city official who offers a toast? To whom is that toast offered?

6. What's different about Marley's Ghost in this film?

7. At what time does the Ghost of Christmas Past arrive?

8. During the Christmas Past sequence, "a poor man" (who's identified that way in the credits) and his wife are seen begging the young Ebenezer not to foreclose on their mortgage. Who plays this poor man? In what later films did he both meet the Devil and make a monkey out of himself?

9. What is Scrooge's fiancée's name?

10. How many brothers does this Ghost of Christmas Present say he has?

11. How does Bob take Tiny Tim to the Cratchit home?

12. What words does Mrs. Cratchit use to describe Scrooge, when her husband proposes a Christmas toast to Ebenezer?

13. Name the song Tiny Tim sings after the Cratchit's toast.

14. During the Ghost of Christmas Yet-to-Come segment, what article of clothing does Scrooge's laundress brag about stealing from Ebenezer? How did she steal it?

15. What does the Ghost of Christmas Yet-to-Come look like? Do you ever see its face?

16. What excuse does Bob Cratchit give Scrooge for coming in late to work the day after Christmas?

17. What is Scrooge's final line in the film? Which *Carol* character usually gets this line of dialogue instead?

A Christmas Carol (1938)

1. This *Christmas Carol* is introduced by the famous Metro-Goldwyn-Mayer logo; the head of a roaring lion, emblazoned with the Latin words "Ars Gratia Artis." Without taking a crash course in dead Romantic languages, can you translate those words into English?

2. What is Scrooge's first line of dialogue?

3. At the beginning of the film, what is Tiny Tim watching that he can't do himself? Who helps him do it?

4. What does Scrooge's nephew Fred give to Bob Cratchit as a Christmas present? What kind?

5. Near the start of the film, Bob Cratchit hands Fred a dirty drinking glass. What was originally in that glass?

6. How much does Scrooge pay Bob Cratchit per week?

7. Why does Scrooge fire Cratchit on Christmas Eve?

8. What's the name of the Christmas carol being sung by the children whom Scrooge passes on his way home from the office?

9. What time does Marley's Ghost visit Scrooge? What time does the Ghost of Christmas Yet-to-Come visit Ebenezer?

10. Joseph L. Mankiewicz produced MGM's version of *A Christmas Carol.* Yet he achieved more fame in another cinematic occupation. Name at least one other well-known Mankiewicz movie. And which films won him back-to-back Oscars?

11. What does Fezziwig, young Scrooge's employer, give the boy as a Christmas present?

12. According to the Ghost of Christmas Present, how many brothers does he have?

13. The Ghost of Christmas Present takes Scrooge to a bakery where the poor go to have their Christmas dinners cooked. How much does that cooking cost?

14. What is contained in the magical horn which the Ghost of Christmas Present carries with him? The one that can stop people from quarreling?

15. Which behind-the-scenes person not only worked on the sentimental holiday movie *A Christmas Carol* but also on *Bride of Frankenstein?* What did he do on both motion pictures?

"God bless us, every one!" A reformed Scrooge lifts the spirits of a happy Tiny Tim.

Goodtimes Home Video box art: Scrooge
(1935—aka A Christmas Carol*).*

16. What story does Bob Cratchit tell his family after their Christmas dinner?

17. Who introduced the Christmas tree to England? When and where?

18. According to this version of the story, what year will Scrooge die if he doesn't change his ways?

19. What's the present that a reformed Scrooge gives to the Cratchit children? (HINT: It's the same one they can all be seen admiring on the Cratchit dinner table at the film's end.)

20. You won't find this information in chapter 5 or in the 1938 film, but which actor had *already played every male part* in *A Christmas Carol* before he appeared in the MGM version? And what part does he perform in the 1938 film?

21. What does the Ghost of Christmas Yet-to-Come look like? Do you ever see its face?

22. What part is played by June Lockhart, who made her film debut in this motion picture? What made her sick while she was doing it?

CHAPTER FIVE
THE SILENT
FILM VERSIONS

The first public performances of *A Christmas Carol* were staged readings by the author, Charles Dickens, who made it something of a holiday tradition to personally narrate the tale for his always-eager audiences. After Dickens's death, copies of his book were printed and passed on to whole new generations of readers, both in Great Britain and America.

This process continued throughout the last half of the nineteenth century. Yet the popularity of Scrooge, Tiny Tim, and the Three Ghosts of Christmas refused to be bound by the barriers of the printed word. And by 1901, *A Christmas Carol* was appearing in artistic mediums undreamed of in 1843.

For what had started as a small book now became adapted for stage productions, sound films, and television shows.

Even silent films.

Unfortunately, little is known about these earliest cinematic adaptations of *A Christmas Carol*. "Unfortunately" because at least *ten* different versions of Dickens's story made it to the silent screen.

What Ye Author knows about them is this:

⚜ The earliest known silent version of *A Christmas Carol* was made in 1901, in England (although there may have been even earlier adaptations; we're swimming in historically murky waters here).

⚜ Subsequent silent adaptations were produced in both American and English studios. There was even a silent *Italian* version, titled *The Dream of Old Scrooge*, made in 1910. This was only ten minutes long.

⚜ Most silent versions were well received by film critics of their day, with the exception of *The Right to Be Happy* (1916). This particular adaptation was made, in America, by Universal Pictures. It was written and directed by Rupert Julian, who also played Scrooge.

Julian's greatest claim to cinematic fame is that he later replaced genius silent director Erich Von Stroheim during the making of Universal's *Merry-Go-Round* (1923), after Von Stroheim was fired by Irving Thalberg, legendary Hollywood producer–a dismissal that apparently was the first time *any* director had been

fired from a Universal picture. (Julian also went on to direct the Lon Chaney *Phantom of the Opera* in 1925). Critics complained that *The Right to Be Happy*, Dickens's English ghost story, had been shot in Southern California!

❄ Perhaps the most interesting silent version of *A Christmas Carol* was the 1913 British production titled *Scrooge*. It starred and was written by Seymour Hicks, who twenty-two years later would also write and star in an all-talking, 1935 British remake of the same picture, examined in chapter 4.

What now follows is a short checklist of all silent *Christmas Carol*s Ye Author could chase down.

A Checklist of Christmas Carol Silent Films

(For further information on these titles, please consult chapter 17, "Credits and Video Sources.")

A Christmas Carol (Great Britain, 1901). Directed by W. R. Booth.

A Christmas Carol (USA, 1908). With: Thomas Ricketts.
This one was made by Essanay, a film production and distribution company that had been started in Chicago in 1907 by George K. Spoor (the "S" of "Essanay"—say it out loud) and G. M. Anderson (The "A"; G. M. was better known as

"Broncho Billy" Anderson). Essanay specialized in slapstick comedies. In 1915, it signed Charlie Chaplin, the legendary Little Tramp. But Chaplin only stayed with the company for one year, and in 1917 Essanay went out of business.

A Christmas Carol (USA, 1910). Directed by Ashley Miller.

A production of the Edison Studios, which was owned and founded by Thomas Alva Edison, a man whom Albert Einstein once called "the greatest inventor of all time" (others have labeled Edison "the greatest thief of all time"—but never mind . . .). Edison also was responsible for the world's first film studio; originally called *The Black Maria*, it was built in 1893.

The Dream of Old Scrooge (Italy, 1910).

Old Scrooge (Italy, 1910).

Although this film is always listed separately in reference books, Ye Author harbors suspicions that it actually may be a retitling of *The Dream of Old Scrooge* (also made in Italy in 1910). However, *The Dream of Old Scrooge* was released March 1910, while *Old Scrooge* was released December 1910. And references indicate that *A Dream of Old Scrooge* was ten minutes long, while *Old Scrooge* clocked in at twelve minutes.

A Christmas Carol (USA, 1912).

Scrooge (Great Britain, 1913). Directed by Leedham Bantock. Written by and starring Sir Seymour Hicks as Scrooge.

A Christmas Carol (Great Britain, 1914). Produced, directed, and written by Harold Shaw. Starring Charles Rock as Scrooge.

The Right to Be Happy (USA, 1916). Written and directed by Rupert Julian. Starring Rupert Julian as Scrooge.

Scrooge (Great Britain, 1922). Written and directed by W. C. Rowden. Starring Russell Thorndike as Scrooge.

TRIVIA QUESTIONS

Silent Film Versions

Due to a scarcity of information on the topic, the upcoming Silent Films Trivia Quiz will be the shortest one in this book.

But that's all right.

Now we have that much more space to explore many *more Christmas Carols*! (Answers on page 219)

1. Name the year of release for the earliest known silent version of *A Christmas Carol*. What country produced this film?

2. Which silent version was criticized for being filmed in Southern California? Give its title and year of release. Also, who played Scrooge in this version?

3. Name two Italian silent versions of *A Christmas Carol* and their year(s) of release.

4. What year was the silent Sir Seymour Hicks version released? What was the title of this version? What did Hicks do on this film?

5. A silent *Christmas Carol* was released by the Essanay company in 1908. Who was this company's biggest star?

6. What was the name of the world's first movie studio? Who built it? When?

7. How many silent film versions of *A Christmas Carol* are listed in this book?

CHAPTER SIX
THE BEST
MADE-FOR-TV VERSION

A CHRISTMAS CAROL
(GREAT BRITAIN, 1984) RATING: ★★★↲

A sumptuously produced, impressively performed, extremely well-directed English adaptation, which combines an admirable fidelity to the original story with new psychological insights into Scrooge's character.

The excellent 1984 *Carol* fell out of the holiday skies like a thunderbolt. Who could have anticipated it? After all, by 1984 the world had already embraced the heartwarming *Mr. Magoo's Christmas Carol*, the upbeat MGM effort, and the magnificent Alastair Sim version. Therefore, there seemed little chance that yet another superior *Carol* would arrive on the scene.

Much less that it would be a version made for television.

A gallery of Dickensian characters from the excellent 1984 made-for-television Christmas Carol: *(clockwise from left) Susannah York as Mrs. Cratchit, George C. Scott as Ebenezer Scrooge, David Warner as Bob Cratchit, Frank Finlay as Marley's Ghost, Roger Rees as Fred Holywell.*

Yet on the night of Monday, December 17, 1984, from eight to ten P.M., CBS broadcast an adaptation which stood head-to-shoulders with the finest *Carols*.

The "George C. Scott" version (so named for the actor who portrays Scrooge) was shot on authentic locations in and around the town of Shrewsbury, England, early in 1984. These locales added a tremendous flavor to the two-hour telefilm: for once, Dickens's story was being played out not on soundstages or sets, but within actual buildings that were standing at the time Dickens published his story. Add these authentic backgrounds to Tony Imi's imaginative cinematography, Roger Murray-Leach's detailed production designs, and Evangeline Harrison's lavish period costumes, and the 1984 *Carol* already begins to show greatness.

But in the final analysis, three key elements make the George C. Scott *Christmas Carol* stand out from the rest: the script, the cast, and the direction.

Written by Roger O. Hirson, the 1984 *Carol* stayed remarkably faithful to the original text, at times lifting entire blocks of dialogue straight out of the book. Yet Hirson was not content to merely transcribe his source material; instead, the writer added extra layers of motivation to Scrooge's character and more fully explored the precise reasons why Ebenezer chose business over humanity.

According to Hirson, those reasons were Scrooge's father and his lost love.

It was in his choice to actually present Scrooge's father on screen (a character who's always *referred* to in the "Christmas Past" sequences of other versions of *Carol* but never, ever *seen*) that Hirson exhibited true inspiration. The 1984 *Carol*

shows that Scrooge's father, here named Silas Scrooge (and portrayed by talented British character actor Nigel Davenport), is a cold, sarcastic, arrogant man who loathed the boyhood Ebenezer and blames the lad for the death of his wife.

Ironically, this childhood rejection saddled the young Scrooge with enormous guilt and sadness. It also transformed him, in adulthood, into a virtual mirror image of the father he hated.

The second, more traditional reason for Scrooge's misanthropy is revealed in the 1984 *Carol* to be the breakup of Ebenezer's engagement to his fiancée Belle (Lucy Gutteridge), who left him when he became so preoccupied with his business that he neglected their relationship. This attention to Belle's rejection is nothing new, of course—in fact, Ebenezer's broken engagement was the motivational engine that drove Albert Finney's *Scrooge*—but rarely has the severe psychic rupture inflicted upon Ebenezer by this breakup been portrayed with such power and emotion.

Yet even Hirson's intelligent attempts to "Freudianize" Scrooge's character would have amounted to very little without the powerful performance of George C. Scott.

Although the sheer bulk and bluster of Scott's performance at times leans uncomfortably close to his equally larger-than-life portrayal of Gen. George Patton, by film's end the actor becomes a truly memorable Scrooge. Aggressively mean, physically imposing, with a simmering rage suggesting a rather dangerous fellow,

Scott's Ebenezer also exhibits fear, tenderness, and self-doubt. There are so many emotional shadings, in fact, that the viewer is left with the impression that Ebenezer's conflicts run very deep indeed.

In any event, Scott's Scrooge is a gem of a performance, perfectly in sync with the psychological emphasis of Hirson's script.

Born George Campbell Scott in 1927 in Wise, Virginia, Scott originally attended the University of Missouri School of Journalism with a desire to become a reporter. But later, Scott switched his emphasis to English and drama and began to act in stage productions. He's reportedly a difficult man to work with, with a well-publicized (former) drinking problem. But George C. Scott is also a man who's never played "the Hollywood game." In fact, this is one star who seems to have nothing but contempt for show business; Scott refused to accept the Best Actor Academy Award he won in 1970 for *Patton*, for example, and turned down an Emmy Award as well. Instead, the man concentrated on giving remarkable performances in such acclaimed motion pictures as *Anatomy of a Murder*, *The Hustler*, and *Dr. Strangelove*. He then became a motion picture and stage director, directing films like *Rage* (1972) and *The Savage Is Loose* (1974), as well as a 1984 Broadway revival of the Noel Coward comedy *Design for Living*.

According to CBS press material surrounding the 1984 *Carol*, Scott said he accepted the role of Scrooge not only for the "challenge and fun," but also for the opportunity to avoid reducing the part to a caricature.

A typically atmospheric shot with Scott as the penurious Scrooge.

Edward Woodward on stilts as the Ghost of Christmas Present accompanies Scott through snowy London streets. Note Woodward's chest wig.

"I think you have to believe in [Scrooge]," the actor was quoted as saying. "If you are going to play him all black in the psychological sense, he'll have a certain one-note quality. [But] . . . if you get into whomever you're playing—I don't care if it's Hitler or Herod the Great—if you believe that this person believes he is right, then you create a more fully rounded human being. Which makes him that much more believable to the audience."

This "believability factor" also extended to a number of other performers. Frank Finlay's ghastly, silver-blue ghost of Jacob Marley is truly otherworldly, while David Warner's Bob Cratchit is the epitome of gentle warmth. Newcomer Anthony Walters makes for an ethereal Tiny Tim, and Susannah York is a tough-yet-tender Mrs. Cratchit (trivia note: two of her own children—Sasha, then eleven, and Orlando, then ten—portrayed two of the Cratchit kids). Also impressive is Michael Carter as the silent, ominous, shroud-draped Ghost of Christmas Yet-to-Come, as is Edward Woodward's robust performance as the Ghost of Christmas Present.

Playing this particular Spirit caused some concern for Woodward, however. For the actor who would later star in the popular eighties television series *The Equalizer* suddenly found himself facing an unusual problem on *A Christmas Carol*: height.

How were the makers of the 1984 *Carol* going to transform the normally 5´10″ Woodward into the 7´6″ Ghost of Christmas of Present? After all, most Present Ghosts are portrayed as tall, physically imposing fellows, whose great exu-

berance is only matched by their towering stature.

The answer?

"Stilts," Edward Woodward revealed in the CBS press kit. "A secret that [director] Clive Donner kept from me until just a couple of days before I was to wear them. You see, the only time I'd ever walked on stilts was when I tried those wooden ones, like the ones in the circus. I could never master those. But the stilts for *A Christmas Carol* were astonishing, actually.

"Basically, they were metal calipers," Woodward continued. "They had ankle joints and knee joints, sort of. So that provided you walked normally, you couldn't fall."

However, finding yourself seven feet in the air doesn't guarantee being able to walk normally. Woodward had to practice a long, uninterrupted stride to make sure he *didn't* tip over. And during one scene, a bit player came too close to Woodward and the Ghost of Christmas Present began to alarmingly weave and wobble!

But problems with metal stilts were nothing compared to Woodward's makeup; fully two hours a day were needed to transform him into the Ghost. This process included adding hairs to a beard Woodward had grown for the part, reddening his cheeks, placing a holly wreath on his head, and draping an enormous robe trimmed in ermine over his shoulders.

Then there was the chest wig.

"The Ghost of Christmas Present is a very virile bloke," said Woodward. "So the producers figured he needed a hairy chest. Unfortunately, I've only got about fourteen hairs on my own chest, and they're all rather precious to me.

"Anyway, when they stuck this chest wig on, it was fine when the glue holding it to me was liquid. But then it started to harden. And the stuff that stuck the wig to my chest began to crack and pull my own hairs out!"

Performances and special effects problems aside, the 1984 *Christmas Carol* is also distinguished by director Clive Donner's admirably sustained period atmosphere and an eerie, supernatural ghostliness. Born January 21, 1926, in London, Donner entered the film business at the tender age of fifteen, first as an assistant editor. In the early 1950s Donner became a full-fledged cutter. In fact, he edited the 1951 *Christmas Carol*! By the mid-fifties he'd begun to direct television commercials, TV series episodes, plays, and feature films.

Clive Donner's most productive period was the 1960s. It was during this decade that he directed an excellent adaptation of the oblique Harold Pinter play *The Caretaker* (1962), as well as the social-climbing black comedy *Nothing but the Best* (1964) and the exaggerated sexual farce *What's New Pussycat?* (1965). But Donner's career then seemed to falter in the seventies and early eighties. Lackluster offerings like *Old Dracula* (1974) and *The Nude Bomb* (1980) unfortunately eclipsed worthier attempts from these decades, such as the tense, made-for-TV thriller *Rogue Male* (1976).

But then he rebounded (in fine form) for *A Christmas Carol*. Donner treat-

Ebenezer Scrooge flanked by the three Spirits from the 1984 Christmas Carol: *Angela Pleasence as the Ghost of Christmas Past, Michael Carter (rear) as the shrouded Ghost of Christmas Yet-to-Come, Edward Woodward as the Ghost of Christmas Present.*

ed this well-worn story with absolute conviction and seriousness, staging each sequence for maximum effectiveness (the Ghost of Christmas Yet-to-Come scenes, as well as the moment when the Ghost of Christmas Present pulls back his robes to reveal the spirits of Ignorance and Want, are especially memorable). Even better, Donner retained Dickens's sense of *humor*. Those who've read *A Christmas Carol* know that the original story has an amusing thread of comedy—and viewers of Donner's version will realize that this is one director who has read that story.

However, it actually wasn't the comedy or even the drama that attracted Clive Donner to *A Christmas Carol*. It was the story's universal appeal, as the following quotes will attest.

"*A Christmas Carol* is about greed and redemption," Donner stated in the CBS presskit. "Who can not relate to that? It also has a wonderful happy ending, which I personally like because it helps dissipate the fear of death and the supernatural, simply by facing up to it."

"And the message within *A Christmas Carol* is still as strong, still as pertinent today as it was when Dickens first wrote it," Edward Woodward added. "This is why I think *all* great literature survives."

"That's certainly a part of *A Christmas Carol*'s lasting appeal," concluded George C. Scott. "The fact that it's a morality play written by a genius writer. But there is another reason. *A Christmas Carol* is a fairy tale. And like all fairy tales, it is eternal.

The Cratchit family, made-for-TV style: Susannah York as Mrs. Cratchit, David Warner as Bob Cratchit. The Cratchit children (left to right) are: Martha (Louise Casser), Tiny Tim (Anthony Walters), Belinda (Sasha York, daughter of Susannah York), little girl Cratchit (Nancy Dodds), Peter (Kieron Hughes), and little boy Cratchit (Orlando Wells, son of Susannah York).

"It all boils down to that one simple thought."

Just as the primary appeal of this handsomely mounted, splendidly performed 1984 *Carol* boils down to two simple words: Great Scott!

TRIVIA QUESTIONS
(Answers on page 220)

A Christmas Carol (1984)

Tiny Tim (Anthony Walters) and Bob Cratchit (David Warner) in a happy moment from the 1984 TV version.

1. On what date was the George C. Scott *Carol* first broadcast? On what network? On what day of the week?

2. Give two reasons Scott agreed to play Scrooge.

3. Where was this version of *A Christmas Carol* filmed?

4. According to Roger O. Hirson's script, which two events in Scrooge's past life irrevocably made him mean?

5. This version gives us a completely new character unseen in any other (TV) version—Scrooge's *father*. What's Scrooge's father's first name? Who plays him? In what other two films did this same actor star with, respectively, killer baboons and intelligent ants?

6. Who plays Tiny Tim in this version? Name at least three other well-known British motion pictures this young actor appeared in before the 1984 *Christmas Carol.*

7. How tall is the actor who played the Ghost of Christmas Present? What's his name? How tall was the Ghost of Christmas Present, and how did the actor playing him get this way? What did this same actor hate most about portraying the Ghost of Christmas Present?

8. Which huge international corporation sponsored the original CBS broadcast of the 1984 *Carol*? This same corporation is best known by a three-initial name. What do those initials mean?

9. What real-life connection did actress Susannah York have with the fictional Cratchit family? What part did York play here?

10. For which American television miniseries did David Warner, who plays Bob Cratchit, win an Emmy?

11. Who composed the 1984 *Carol's* musical score?

12. What unusual *religious* award did the 1984 *Carol* win in 1985?

13. George C. Scott saved his soul in *A Christmas Carol*. In what other film was he partially responsible for destroying the world?

14. At the end of the original broadcast of *A Christmas Carol,* actor George C. Scott appeared out of character in a brief segment titled "Read All About It." A joint project between CBS and the Library of Congress, this educational segment alerted viewers to several books about Charles Dickens and Christmas that had been recommended by the Library of Congress. Name one of these books.

CHAPTER SEVEN
OTHER TELEVISION VERSIONS

Among the most interesting *Christmas Carols* are those specifically tailored for television.

Some have been feature-length versions. Some, one-hour specials. Some have updated the story into contemporary surroundings, or reworked Dickens's plot to fit the particular demands of an ongoing TV series.

Yet the outstanding characteristic of the many produced-for-TV *Christmas Carol*s is their sheer *volume*; quite a few more *Carols* have been made for television than adapted for the big screen.

Not all of these TV versions are still available for viewing, however. And not all have been good.

What *is* available, and what now follows, is a listing of all the produced-for-TV versions Ye Author was able to catalog for *The "Christmas Carol" Trivia Book*, a checklist which comes with the following instructions:

1. Where *A Christmas Carol* has been televised as a stand-alone TV special, it has been noted as such.

2. If it has been televised as an episode of an ongoing television series, the episode title (if available) is listed before the series title.

3. If an episode title is not available, then just the name of the series on which that *Carol* adaptation was televised is listed.

4. Also listed are all *Christmas Carol* television movies. These are rated the same way a theatrical *Christmas Carol* motion picture would be; that is, from one to four stars, with four stars being best.

5. As for chronology, the month, day, and year any particular *Carol* was first televised is noted if such information was available; month and year only if it was not.

6. Critical information and historical commentary are appended to certain key titles.

7. While Ye Author is certain he hasn't listed *every* televised version, he has tried to gather all the American and English TV adaptations of *A Christmas Carol* he's aware of.

8. Some of these titles are preceded by an asterisk (*). This symbol simply means that that version is described at greater length elsewhere in this book; the chapter that information appears in is indicated in parenthesis at the end of the title.

9. For further information on who made and starred in these productions, please refer to the "Credits" section in this book (chapter 17).

At which point you're thoroughly confused, correct?

Never mind. The notational system used here will become much easier to comprehend once you've started using it.

A Checklist of Produced-for-Television Christmas Carols

Christmas Carol. Broadcast from television station WBKB, Chicago. December 1945.

Christmas Carol, A. Broadcast from WABD, New York, for the Dumont Network. December 25, 1947. John Carradine was Scrooge in this one.

"Christmas Carol, A" (on *Philco Television Playhouse*). NBC. December 19, 1948. Dennis King played Scrooge.

Dickens's Christmas Carol. Broadcast on the ABC Network from New York. December 24, 1948. Puppet version with Rupert Rose Marionettes.

"Christmas Carol, A" (on *Fireside Theater*). NBC. December 25, 1951.

An early adaptation starring Sir Ralph Richardson, Arthur Treacher, Melville Cooper, and Malcolm Keene.

"Christmas Carol, A" (on *Kraft Television Theatre*). NBC. December 24, 1952.

Another early version, this one starring Malcolm Keene and Harry Townes as Scrooge and Bob Cratchit, respectively.

"Christmas Carol, A" (on *Kraft Television Theatre*). NBC. December 24, 1953.

Kraft Theatre must have been pleased with their 1952 broadcast of the Dickens classic, for they mounted yet another version a year later. The stars this time were Melville Cooper as Scrooge, Noel Leslie, Denis Greene, Harry Townes (again), Geoffrey Lumb, and Valerie Cossart.

"Spirit of Christmas, The" (on *Shower of Stars*). CBS. December 23, 1954. RATING: ***

This surprisingly good adaptation—if one takes into account the year it was made and the medium for which it was made—was originally broadcast in color. Unfortunately, all existing videos reproduce the show in black-and-white. But that's a minor annoyance in what is otherwise an entertaining, if somewhat naive, musical interpretation by Maxwell Anderson of the Dickens classic.

"The Spirit of Christmas" was first broadcast as an episode of a CBS variety-anthology program titled *Shower of Stars*, which alternated with *Climax!* This series was hosted by actor William Lundigan and sponsored by the Chrysler

Corporation. In fact, the Viking Video Classics tape of this show includes a number of commercials which originally ran with the program. These are almost worth the price of a rental alone; the advertisements relentlessly extol the virtues of owning a brand-new Plymouth, Dodge, DeSoto, Chrysler, or "exclusive Imperial" automobile.

The one-hour presentation itself is a fairly elaborate one, especially for the days of early television. There are sturdy sets and professional production values, which resemble shows produced a good ten years later (although near the end of the program, for a shot where star Fredric March sits at a table listening to a *very long* song, director Ralph Levy holds a tight closeup of the actor's face for what seems like an eternity).

March, a respected thespian who was a cowinner in the Best Actor category for the 1932 Academy Awards, plays Scrooge with a scowl, a hank of long, stringy hair, and a false hooked nose that makes him look a bit like a vulture (this nose also looks like it was in constant danger of melting under the hot studio lights). The actor makes for a lively, energetic curmudgeon, a shouter who bellows out every "Bah, humbug!" with real gusto.

Playing Marley's Ghost is Basil Rathbone, the evil Sheriff of Nottingham from the Errol Flynn-starring *Robin Hood*. Rathbone portrays Marley as an agonized, semitransparent phantom with cobwebbed fingers; he's a tormented ghost in acute spiritual pain. It's also a slightly hammy performance, but not offensively so.

As for technical credits, this comedy-drama-musical extravaganza was pep-

pered with numerous a cappella songs performed by the Roger Wagner Chorale, a then-popular vocal group. The adaptation and lyrics for these melodies were written by playwright Maxwell Anderson, whose songs are actually of a *higher* caliber than the tunes heard in either the 1970 *Scrooge* or the 1992 *Muppet Christmas Carol* (though not as good as the songs in *Mr. Magoo's Christmas Carol*).

Equally interesting, musically, is the fact that "The Spirit of Christmas" was scored by Bernard Herrmann. A respected Hollywood composer whose first sound-track was done for Orson Welles's *Citizen Kane* (and who is best known for his scores for such Alfred Hitchcock classics as *Psycho*, *Vertigo*, and *North by Northwest*), Herrmann's "Christmas" music sounds suspiciously like a hodgepodge of cues taken from his previous film work. Nevertheless, there's no denying that Herrmann's "Spirit of Christmas" score is an eminently listenable one, particularly during the ghostly graveyard scene, which features atonal chords and moaning choruses on the soundtrack.

Amusingly, the Ghost of Christmas Yet-to-Come is played in the graveyard scene by a mynah bird. A true *Christmas Carol* first!

If you can get into the—ah—*spirit* of the thing, "The Spirit of Christmas" is a great way to reexperience a primitive yet honorable era of fifties television. Professional, innocent, and smooth, this is a perfect example of an early primetime special, complete with name stars and mellow musical numbers (not to mention Chrysler commercials!).

"The Spirit of Christmas," then, is an earnest, unpretentious offering that only wants to entertain its Wonder Bread/Eisenhower-era audience; one made during a time when it was still a grand occasion for the entire family to gather around their brand-new television set.

Eye On New York. December 1955.

Featured a contemporary update of *A Christmas Carol.*

"Stingiest Man in Town, The" (on *The Alcoa Hour*). NBC. December 23, 1956.

This ninety-minute musical version starred Basil Rathbone as Scrooge. Two years earlier, he had played Marley's Ghost in another musical version, the CBS *Shower of Stars* episode titled "The Spirit of Christmas" (see entry number 8 on this list). Vic Damone was young Scrooge in this one, and it's apparently available on videotape–although that tape is *so* hard to find, Ye Author can't even determine which label it's on!

"Trail to Christmas, The" (on *The General Electric Theater*). CBS. December 15, 1957.

A westernized "cowboy *Christmas Carol*," which featured Richard Eyer (the genie from *The 7th Voyage of Sinbad*), John McIntire as a guy named Scrooge, and James Stewart–the star of the *other* best-known Christmas film, *It's a Wonderful Life!* Stewart also directed this version.

* Mr. Magoo's Christmas Carol. December 18, 1962. (See chapter 7.)

Christmas Carol, A (English). Broadcast by the BBC, from London. December 1962.

Carol for Another Christmas. ABC. December 28, 1964.

Twilight Zone creator Rod Serling wrote this strange contemporary version of *A Christmas Carol*, just two years after the Cuban missile crisis. That recent event was mirrored in the plot, which showed a world headed toward nuclear destruction.

The incredible cast included Sterling Hayden as Daniel Grudge, an isolationist, *Scrooge*-like cynic, Ben Gazzara (as Hayden's idealistic nephew Fred Grudge), Eva Marie Saint, Percy Rodriques, and Peter Sellers (as "The Imperial Me: King of Individualists"). Steve Lawrence, Pat Hingle, and Robert Shaw played, respectively, the Ghosts of Past, Present, and Future. Henry Mancini did the music. Joseph L. Mankiewicz–who produced the 1938 MGM version of *A Christmas Carol*–directed.

Unfortunately, this tantalizing curio is not yet on videotape.

Mr. Scrooge. December 1964.

* Christmas Carol, A. Animated special from Australia. CBS. December 13, 1970. (See chapter 13.)

* Christmas Carol, A. Animated special. ABC. December 21, 1971. (See chapter 11.)

Christmas Present. Broadcast by the BBC. December 1975.

This British, made-for-TV feature starred Peter Chelsom as "Nigel Playfayre," a Scrooge-surrogate who undergoes the usual spiritual eye-opening. *Revenge of the Creature Features Movie Guide* describes it as a "gentle, mild-mannered TV movie, written-directed by Tony Bicat." It also starred Bill Fraser.

Rich Little's Christmas Carol. Broadcast by the CBC (Canadian Broadcasting Corporation). December 9, 1978. RATING: * *

This shot-on-videotape, one-hour special was aired by the Canadian Broadcasting Corporation during the Christmas season of 1978. And while it's a fairly faithful adaptation of Dickens's classic, it's not much of an entertainment, and wasn't shown in the United States for years.

The gimmick here certainly sounds promising. Comedian Rich Little performs all the major parts of the *Carol* by impersonating various celebrities, who then act as the characters in the story. For instance, Little's W. C. Fields—complete with top hat, gray hair, fat suit, and false nose—is Scrooge. Little also impersonates Humphrey Bogart, who portrays the Ghost of Christmas Past.

But what looks good on paper doesn't always jell in production.

To begin with, *Rich Little's Christmas Carol* suffers from a mundane script, which includes such tired old gags as Fields opening the sock where he hides his

money only to see moths fly out. Also, Paul Lynde appears as a goofy Bob Cratchit, acting very much as he did on the *Hollywood Squares* show.

Furthermore, there's an obnoxious, omnipresent laugh track and loads of silly slapstick. Most damaging of all, the whole thing isn't very funny.

The producers of *Rich Little's Christmas Carol* probably thought that the basic *idea* of Rich Little impersonating various characters acting out the *Carol* was hilarious in itself. Yet while it's certainly interesting watching Little pretend to be such stars as Groucho Marx, John Wayne, Laurel and Hardy, George Burns, and Cary Grant, *Rich Little's Christmas Carol* is ultimately a stale, one-joke enterprise that would hardly pass muster as a Vegas lounge act.

Nicely produced, definitely a 1970s-era curio. Also, alas, for *Carol* completists only.

"Stingiest Man in Town, The." Animated special. NBC. December 23, 1978.

Rankin/Bass cartoon featuring the voices of Walter Matthau as Scrooge, with Tom Bosley, Theodore Bikel, Dennis Day, Debra Clinger, Robert Morse, and others.

American Christmas Carol, An. ABC. December 16, 1979. RATING: * * 1/2

This made-for-TV movie update, set in a small Depression-era New Hampshire town, features former *Happy Days* star Henry Winkler as a surrogate-Scrooge named Benedict Slade, an elderly banker who, in his youth, heartlessly betrayed the kindly furniture manufacturer who took him in. Slade then amassed a fortune by preying on the misfortunes of his fellow townspeople. He now has the power to reopen a local granite quarry, which will provide much-needed jobs for the town's citizens.

But Slade won't. Instead, he's visited by the specter of his old business partner and three Ghosts (portrayed as townspeople lookalikes, all of whom owe Slade money). These Spirits ultimately persuade Slade to reopen the quarry, of course. Slade also proves his newfound goodness by adopting a needy orphan boy.

There are some good touches in this adaptation. Winkler brings a muffled despair to his part, although his characterization definitely lacks the vigor of, say, a Scott or a Sim. The 1930s milieu is also nicely evoked through carefully reproduced costumes and hairstyles. And the town's wintry environment is appropriately dour: snowy, overcast, and gray. Also worth noting is Slade's transition into his own Christmas Past, which is heralded by a bedside radio that suddenly announces news-flashes from forty years ago. Best of all is the elaborate makeup, which transforms Winkler from a vital youth into a tired old man.

Henry Winkler as Scrooge-surrogate Benedict Slade in An American Christmas Carol *(1979). Makeup by Rick Baker.*

But this shot-in-Toronto production ultimately suffers from a noticeable lack of passion. Everything about it is hushed and restrained, an approach which certainly evokes a downbeat atmosphere, but doesn't exactly generate high drama.

Blessed with an imaginative script, cursed with pedestrian direction (by Eric Till), this drab, low-key *Carol* is an interesting attempt at modernizing Dickens's classic. Unfortunately, and despite the fact that it's never boring, this is one *Christmas Carol* that never catches fire, either.

* *Christmas Carol, A.* Dance version. Broadcast on The Entertainment Channel (cable). December 5, 1982. (See chapter 15.)

* *Christmas Carol, A.* Australian animated special. Broadcast through Syndication. November 1984. (See chapter 13.)

* *Christmas Carol, A.* CBS. (George C. Scott version) December 17, 1984. (See chapter 6.)

"Christmas Carol II: The Sequel" (on *George Burns Comedy Week*). CBS. December 11, 1985.

 George Burns Comedy Week was a short-lived 1985 anthology show on CBS. It only lasted thirteen episodes, and was produced by comedian Steve Martin, as well as writer-director Carl Gottlieb. The premise consisted of a cigar-smoking George Burns introducing new stories each week, comical tales whose stars, plots, settings, and premises changed with every episode.

 The highpoint of this enterprise was the thirty-minute-long "Christmas Carol II: The Sequel." James Whitmore starred as a very different sort of Scrooge. Revisited by Marley's Ghost one year after their initial encounter, Scrooge has a newfound humility and generosity that causes Marley to criticize him—because now philanthropic Ebenezer has turned into a champion wimp!

 This funny adaptation also starred Roddy McDowall as Bob Cratchit and Ed

Begley Jr. as a *very* adult Tiny Tim. Not yet available on videotape.

* **"Jetson Christmas Carol, A"** (on *The Jetsons*). ABC. December 1985. (See chapter 13.)

John Grin's Christmas. ABC. December 6, 1986.

A contemporary hour-long reworking of the story that has the unusual distinction of being an all-black *Carol*. Robert Guillaume directed and starred as the titled, Scrooge-like toymaker. Roscoe Lee Browne, Geoffrey Holder, Ted Lange, and Kevin Guillaume also appeared. Not yet on video.

Christmas at the Movies. Syndicated. November 1990.

Hosted by Gene Kelly, this one-hour syndicated special celebrated all things Christmasy. Beginning with a clip from the 1905 Edison silent film "The Nite Before Christmas," *Christmas at the Movies* then examined various cinematic manifestations of the holiday which appeared in the twentieth century. It culminated in excerpts from the romance/comedy *When Harry Met Sally*.

Not a *Christmas Carol*-themed program as such, and therefore a bit out of the scope of this book. However, *Christmas at the Movies* did include a section on various actors who've played Scrooge. Among the featured performers were Sir Seymour Hicks, Rich Little, Mr. Magoo, and Henry Winkler. Available on Columbia Tri-Star Home Video.

TRIVIA QUESTIONS
(Answers on page 221)

Other Television Versions

1. What's the title of the earliest known version of *A Christmas Carol* broadcast on American television? In what year and from what city did it originate?

2. Name the title and year of the only "cowboy *Carol*" in this book. Which of its stars also appeared in *It's a Wonderful Life!*

An American Christmas Carol (1979)

3. Although *An American Christmas Carol* supposedly takes place in an American small town during the Depression, it was actually filmed in a foreign country. Name the shooting locale, as well the name of the town, the state and the year where/when *An American Christmas Carol* supposedly takes place.

4. Give the full name of the Scrooge-like manufacturer here. Which actor plays him?

5. Instead of money, what does Slade give to the orphans who come caroling to his door?

6. Instead of "Humbug!" what is Slade's favorite expression?

7. What action does Slade perform in his warehouse basement that immediately precedes a ghostly visit by his dead partner?

8. The Fezziwig character is called Mr. Brewster here. What kind of business does Brewster operate?

9. What's the full name of Slade's business?

10. What is the full name of the Tiny Tim character here, and by what nickname does Tim's father call him? What disease does this Tiny Tim surrogate have?

11. Describe what the Ghost of Christmas Yet-to-Come looks like. What is he called in this version? Does he speak?

12. Who did the makeup that turned the young Henry Winkler into the old Benedict Slade?

Carol for Another Christmas (1964)

13. Who wrote this special? For what other television show is this writer primarily known?

14. What danger faced the world in this contemporary update of Dickens's classic?

15. Who played Scrooge in this version? What was his character's name?

George Burns Comedy Week (1985)

16. Name the actors who played the wimpy Scrooge and the grown-up Tiny Tim in this comedy *Carol* "sequel."

John Grin's Christmas (1986)

17. What actor played the Scrooge-like toymaker here?

18. How is this *Christmas Carol* different from all others?

Rich Little's Christmas Carol (1978)

19. Impressionist Rich Little plays virtually all the major roles in this TV special— but usually as *other* famous movie personalities. Which cynical 1930s comedian does Little impersonate for the role of Scrooge?

20. What is the ersatz Scrooge's business in this version?

21. What politician does Little impersonate for Marley's Ghost? Instead of chains and money boxes, what's wrapped around this apparition?

22. What is inside the waterbed on which W. C. Fields sleeps?

23. Which celebrity writer does Little impersonate to play Tiny Tim?

24. What does the Ghost of Christmas Yet-to-Come look like? Does it talk?

Shower of Stars: "The Spirit of Christmas" (1954)

25. Name the television series on which "The Spirit of Christmas" was first broadcast. Who was the host?

26. Was this musical broadcast in color or black-and-white?

27. What new Chrysler cars are proudly promoted during the show?

28. Who plays both Fred and the Ghost of Christmas Present?

29. Who wrote the music? Name this famous composer's first film.

30. When and where was Basil Rathbone born? What year did he die?

31. What does Marley's Ghost remove from its chains to show Scrooge? (HINT: It has something to do with their partnership.)

32. How does Scrooge know he hasn't imagined Marley's Ghost?

33. Name the film for which Fredric March was the cowinner of a Best Actor Academy Award. When did this happen? Who was the *other* winner of the Best Actor award that year? For what film?

34. What does the Ghost of Christmas Present do after he backs Scrooge up under the mistletoe?

35. What does the Ghost of Future Yet-to-Come look like?

36. What date of death is on Scrooge's tombstone?

37. Where does Ebenezer get the sprig of holly that he hangs on his "Scrooge & Marley" sign near program's end?

38. At the end of the program, William Lundigan introduces actress Barbara Hale (who played Della Street to Raymond Burr's *Perry Mason*) and asks her to talk about an upcoming episode of the alternating *Climax!* By what nickname does Lundigan address Hale?

39. What's the major packaging error seen on the front cover of the Viking Video Classics videocassette box of "The Spirit of Christmas"?

CHAPTER EIGHT
THE BIG-BUDGET MUSICAL VERSION

SCROOGE (GREAT BRITAIN, 1970) RATING: ★★★

A lavish production with numerous songs, impressive sets, and elaborately choreographed crowd scenes, *Scrooge* (1970) boasts a good title performance by Albert Finney and an admirable fidelity toward its original source material.

There *is* a problem with this musical, though. And it's a big one.

The songs aren't very good.

Which is sort of like eating a hamburger and discovering that the only bad thing about it is the meat.

Scrooge was produced by an American, Robert F. Solo, a former talent agent and studio executive who became an independent producer (responsible for

both the 1978 and 1993 remakes of *Invasion of the Body Snatchers,* among other works). It was photographed by Oswald Morris, a prolific, highly regarded British cinematographer, who had already lensed such visually memorable projects as *Moby Dick, Moulin Rouge,* and *The Spy Who Came in From the Cold.* The director of *Scrooge* was Ronald Neame, a then-fifty-nine-year-old Englishman who had begun his career as a cameraman (*In Which We Serve, Blithe Spirit*) before directing such quietly effective works as *The League of Gentlemen* and *The Prime of Miss Jean Brodie.* Most interesting of all is that the same Ronald Neame also served as a producer to director David Lean's classic Charles Dickens adaptations, *Great Expectations* (for which Neame also cowrote the screenplay) and *Oliver Twist.*

But then there's the man who wrote the songs, Leslie Bricusse (pronounced BRICK-us).

Ye Author distinctly remembers a sinking feeling in the pit of his stomach when, during this film's initial theatrical run in 1970, he first spied Bricusse's name among *Scrooge's* opening credits. After all, this was the same man who'd composed listless tunes for the eminently forgettable *Doctor Dolittle, Stop the World, I Want to Get Off* and the 1969 remake of *Goodbye, Mr. Chips.*

True to form, Bricusse's work on *Scrooge* is equally undistinguished. While two tunes do linger in the memory–"I Like Life" and "Thank You Very Much"–Ye Author would be very surprised if anyone were humming these songs after the end

Albert Finney as Scrooge.

of this movie. Even worse, *Scrooge*'s melodies constantly interrupt the storyline, becoming progressively more irritating as the plot unfolds. In fact, it's not long before one begins to anticipate the next song with dread; you *know* it's going to stop the narrative dead in its tracks.

However, Bricusse also contributed a surprisingly effective *screenplay* for *Scrooge*. All of Dickens's high points are handled well; Bricusse even throws in a creative moment, when Scrooge (literally) goes to Hell. It's in these infernal regions that a uniquely sardonic Marley (Alec Guinness, in an amusing, self-parodying performance) terrifies Ebenezer by showing him a *frozen* reproduction of the offices of Scrooge & Marley. "You'll be the only chilly man in Hell," Marley diabolically points out.

Other laudable points about *Scrooge* include the impressive opening credits, which were painted by the then-trendy English artist Ronald Searle. Furthermore, the young actor playing Tiny Tim (Richard Beaumont) is refreshingly free of the "cutes" (our first introduction to Tim, by the way, has him wistfully staring into a toy shop window in a scene that echoes a far more magical moment in the 1951 *Christmas Carol*; the Sim version had a toy shop window display that consisted of marvelous—and authentic—Victorian-era mechanical dolls). And *Scrooge* avoids excessive Hollywood sentimentality. It's a clear-eyed treatment of a time-honored story, straightforward and disciplined, marked by Neame's mature craftsmanship.

Tom Jenkins (Anton Rodgers, standing on coffin) helps a joyous crowd of Ebenezer's debtors celebrate Scrooge's death.

Until Bricusse's songs come along . . .

However, the best thing about this picture—as is usually the case—is the man playing Scrooge.

Albert Finney—born in 1936 in Salford, England—was the son of a Lancashire bookmaker. He won a scholarship to the Royal Academy of the Dramatic Arts in 1956 and devoted himself to the stage, ultimately understudying Laurence Olivier during a season at Stratford-on-Avon. His first major film role came as a working-class rebel in the 1960 "kitchen sink drama" *Saturday Night and Sunday Morning*. Finney then scored a huge international success as the lead in *Tom Jones* (1963). Finney later formed a film production company called Memorial Enterprises, which released such artistic successes as the 1968 counter-culture hit *If* . . .

Albert Finney also went on to become artistic director for the Royal Court Theater, staying close to his stage-bound roots. Over the ensuing decades he's achieved international renown for roles in a wide variety of films. Such as *Murder on the Orient Express* (as Hercule Poirot), *Annie* (as Daddy Warbucks), and *Shoot the Moon*.

Ah, but how is Finney in *Scrooge*?

To be blunt, a bit hammy. But only *slightly* so. Finney obviously had a good time with this role; his Ebenezer is a sour, hunched-over figure, lips twisted in a perpetual sneer, hands cramped by years of counting money. There's also some-

Albert Finney as Scrooge balances his books.

thing in Finney's angry stare that makes you suspect that this is one Scrooge capable of physical violence. As for his singing . . . well, Albert Finney may be frequently off-key, but at least he's enthusiastic.

He was also relatively young to be playing Scrooge. Finney was only thirty-three when he played Scrooge (you can see what he really looked like back in 1970 during the Christmas Past sequence, when the young Ebenezer courts the fiancée who will reject him). Therefore, an elaborate makeup was devised to artificially age the actor. It took a full two hours, each day, to transform Finney into a wrinkled old man.

This process began by making a plaster cast of the actor's head, on which approximately fifty rubber "bald caps" were molded, caps which could then be used as backups throughout the filming of the production. Next, Finney's hair was flattened down. Then one of the bald caps was placed over it. Now a wig of wispy hair was attached on top of the cap, and plastic "skin" was applied around Finney's eyes and on his hands, to wrinkle them. The final touch was to stain Finney's teeth yellow.

Once his makeup was complete, Finney studied the original John Leech illustrations of the first edition *Christmas Carol* for inspiration on how to physically interpret the part. The actor decided that Scrooge should have a shaky, unsteady walk; also, Finney employed various vocal tricks he'd learned in the theater to suggest a hint of wispy hollowness in Ebenezer's voice.

The big budget musical version of Tiny Tim and Bob Cratchit. Richard Beaumont (left) and David Collings.

The final result of these labors had 1970 film critics predicting that Albert Finney would certainly be nominated for a Best Actor Oscar for portraying Scrooge. Surprisingly, he wasn't. But Finney *did* win a 1970 Golden Globe Award for Best Actor in a Musical Comedy.

Here's a few other interesting behind-the-scenes tidbits concerning *Scrooge*:

Albert Finney out of makeup as a younger Ebenezer romancing his financée (Suzanne Neve) in Scrooge.

- The elaborate sets, designed by Terry Marsh, were based on old lithographs of the Victorian period.

- An impressive "Hell Set" was specifically built for the scene where Scrooge goes to Hades. But production designer Marsh resolutely shied away from conventional ideas of Hell. He instead visualized a huge red cavern studded with agonized faces that protruded from the rock, and placed that cavern within the gaping jaws of a monstrous dragon. After it was then built, the Hell Set filled an entire sound stage. It utilized twenty tons of timber, forty tons of plaster, a dozen miles of steel, four hundred gallons of paint, and five hundred sacks of red cork chippings (which were used to represent glowing embers) for its construction materials. The Hell Set was also populated by five twelve-inch-long rats, carefully guarded by a member of the art department whom the crew affectionately nicknamed "The Rat Man."

- Dame Edith Evans, who portrays the Ghost of Christmas Past, was costumed with specific clothing that would suggest a sort of "eternal grandmother."

❋ The strange, broken-hip walk of Marley's Ghost was invented by Alec Guinness, who was suspended from overhead wires during most of his scenes so that Marley would constantly seem to be bobbing up and down like a balloon—an apparition that would sail off into the air if it weren't held down by chains.

Alec Guinness as Marley's Ghost.

In the final analysis, however, even with these interesting touches, *Scrooge* is too long and draggy to inspire any sort of wholehearted critical endorsement. It starts off well enough, and viewers who just want to see something splashy will certainly get their (rental) money's worth. But one can't help wishing that *Scrooge*'s producers had simply dropped their song-and-dance numbers and concentrated on the story instead.

Incidentally, producer Robert Solo must have been a little worried about those numbers even before his film was released. Just witness the response he gave to Clyde Gilmour of the *Toronto Telegram*, when pressed on the "plain-vanilla" flavor of *Scrooge*'s songs:

"We *never* wanted the songs to stand out or become Hit Parade chart-climbers," Solo said. "We wanted them integrated into the film. We did *not* set out to turn this into a typical Hollywood musical."

Unfortunately, a typical Hollywood musical is exactly what Solo got.

TRIVIA QUESTIONS
(Answers on page 224)

Scrooge

Ebenezer and the Ghost of Christmas Yet-to-Come (Paddy Stone) visit Scrooge's grave.

1. Who was the artist responsible for the hand-drawn titles which open *Scrooge*?

2. Who wrote the screenplay?

3. What is the first song we hear after the film's opening credits?

4. At what time does Fred come to visit Uncle Ebenezer in his office?

5. When Bob Cratchit is at the toy shop window with his children, how much money does he say he has in his pockets? What is the cost of the apples he buys his children?

6. According to this version, how long has Jacob Marley been dead?

7. How long did it take to apply Albert Finney's old-age makeup?

8. What does Scrooge pick up to defend himself with when his door begins to open to admit Marley's ghost?

9. What does Marley's Ghost sit down on during his visit with Scrooge?

10. When asked by the Ghost of Christmas Past why he didn't join in with

Fezziwig's Christmas dance, what excuse does Ebenezer give?

11. What is Scrooge's fiancée's name in this version? Where does she place her engagement ring after she's taken it off her finger?

12. What year does this version of *A Christmas Carol* take place?

13. How many brothers does this Ghost of Christmas Present say he has?

14. What does the Ghost of Christmas Present give Scrooge to drink? (HINT: It's in a huge golden chalice).

15. What is the main course of the Cratchit's Christmas dinner?

16. What does the Ghost of Christmas Yet-to-Come look like in this version? Do you ever see its face? If so, what does it look like?

17. Who played the Ghost of Christmas Yet-to-Come in this version? Did he have another job on this film?

18. The Ghost of Christmas-Yet-to-Come shows Scrooge a huge crowd of former debtors gathered around the latter's office, celebrating the fact that Ebenezer is dead. Name the man who's the leader of this crowd and describe what job he has.

19. When Marley meets Scrooge in Hell, what job does Jacob say Lucifer has in mind for Ebenezer?

A reformed miser picks out a Christmas gift for Tiny Tim: Albert Finney as Scrooge.

20. What costume does Scrooge dress up in near the end of the film?

21. What does Scrooge hang on his door knocker at the finale?

22. A real curve ball here, since Ye Author didn't previously mention this. But who was *originally* approached for the role of *Scrooge*, before Albert Finney accepted the part?

Dressed in his Father Christmas suit, Albert Finney leads the closing song and dance number of Scrooge.

CHAPTER NINE
THE FUNNIEST VERSION

BLACKADDER'S CHRISTMAS CAROL (GREAT BRITAIN, 1988) RATING: ★★★

There's no Jacob Marley, only one Ghost, and Ebenezer Scrooge is actually "the kindliest and loveliest man in all England."

Despite these radical alterations, however, *Blackadder's Christmas Carol* is still the most inventive—and hilarious—adaptation covered in this book.

Or, to put it more succinctly—the most *deviant* adaptation!

Ebenezer Blackadder (Rowan Atkinson, who played a befuddled priest in *Four Weddings and a Funeral*) is a cheerful shopkeeper who lives in Victorian London with his bumbling assistant Baldrick (Tony Robinson). On Christmas Eve, after suffering through a never-ending parade of screeching relatives, idiot employ-

ees, and overweight orphans (all of whom manage to steal Blackadder's few Christmas presents), the tired but still kind-hearted Ebenezer goes to bed.

Then he's visited by a drunken Christmas Ghost (Robbie Coltrane), who kicks down Blackadder's bedchamber door to show him three generations of relatives—Blackadder's past, present, and future—who all were or will be scheming, sarcastic crooks.

The future vision holds a special significance. Ebenezer learns that if he mends his goodly ways and becomes a dirty, rotten scoundrel, his relatives will rule the universe. Otherwise, the Blackadder-Yet-to-Come will wind up as a worthless slave, one forced to wear a leather jock strap.

Convinced that his former good works were the actions of a fool, the "nicest man in England" wakes up on Christmas morning determined to become "the horridest man in the world." His first bad deed? Allowing Baldrick to nibble only on the wishbone from Blackadder's Christmas turkey.

A wishbone without any meat on it.

This short (forty-three minutes), side-splitting inversion of Dickens's classic turns *A Christmas Carol* right on its head. It was based on a successful late eighties BBC-TV comedy show called *Blackadder*, a satire on the Middle Ages that chronicled Atkinson's wickedly funny misadventures as the perpetually scheming Duke of Edinburgh, *aka* "The Black Adder." This particular episode was originally broadcast in England during the 1988 holiday season.

At root, *Blackadder's Christmas Carol* plays like an extended Monty Python sketch. And like Python before it, the humor is mainly verbal. Insults, non sequiturs, and wisecracks abound; for instance, if you listen carefully to the sweet mock-Christmas song that opens the show, you'll hear carolers joyfully proclaim that "Ebenezer Blackadder is sickeningly good" and "he doesn't laugh at toilet humor." Plus, Ebenezer only says "Humbug" once. Yet this exclamation is treated as a cheery Christmas greeting (which it is)! And the show is filled with goofy catch phrases such as, "Well, baste my steaming pudding!"

Blackadder's Christmas Carol isn't only about verbal comedy, however. The production values are quite good for a shot-on-videotape production, and Atkinson is wickedly funny as the viper-mouthed "Bad Adders" (he and Robinson portray their own relatives). Yet the show really shines when it gleefully deconstructs classic bits from Dickens's original story. Such as having the Christmas Ghost explain to the kindly Ebenezer that this Spirit was on his rounds to reform old misers, "but you're such an obviously good bloke I'm wasting my time here."

So expect something saucy, snide, and irreverent. Guest-starring Queen Victoria. With side trips to the Elizabethan, Regency, and "Space Age" periods (where everybody mouths nonsensical sci-fi babble). Plus tons of blue humor about bottoms, bodily functions, and fat people. Not to mention Three Enormous Orphans.

Video box art for Blackadder's Christmas Carol.

As you've probably guessed by now, *Blackadder's Christmas Carol* isn't for everyone. But for fans of sophisticated or just plain silly humor, who enjoy similarly sarcastic shows like *Fawlty Towers*, this *is* a broad, enjoyable spoof that delights in its twisted efforts to offend.

As well as the perfect antidote for those who've overdosed on Christmas's sweetness and light.

TRIVIA QUESTIONS
(Answers on page 225)

Blackadder's Christmas Carol

1. What sort of business does Ebenezer Blackadder run? Where is it located?

2. What has to replace the Baby Jesus in Baldrick's nativity play, and why?

3. Here's an easy one—who plays Blackadder?

4. *Blackadder's Christmas Carol* delights in giving Dickens's original characters some new and rather novel names. For instance, what are Mrs. Cratchit and Tiny Tim called?

5. Who is the Big Pink Pixie in the Sky?

6. How does the Christmas Ghost enter Blackadder's bed chamber?

7. What is the name of Blackadder's evil ancestor in the Elizabethan period (the first ancestor shown to Ebenezer by the Christmas Ghost)?

8. Who plays both Queen Elizabeth and Queen Asphyxia IX?

9. What costume do both Blackadder and Baldrick wind up wearing in the court of Queen Asphyxia?

10. In what three periods of time does the Christmas Ghost show Blackadder visions of the past and future?

11. After the previously benevolent Blackadder turns mean, he's visited by his giggling, foolish niece. What does he say she's blessed with?

12. What do Queen Victoria and Prince Albert do every Christmas to keep in touch with the poor?

13. What do Victoria and Albert offer Blackadder as a reward for being so good?

14. What does Blackadder call the astonished Queen Victoria when she arrives to present him with the reward mentioned in question 13?

15. What part of his Christmas turkey does Blackadder give Baldrick at the end of the story?

CHAPTER TEN
THE BEST MUSICAL VERSION

MR. MAGOO'S CHRISTMAS CAROL (USA, 1962) RATING: ★★★★

Mr. *Magoo's Christmas Carol* was first unveiled to the American general public on December 18, 1962, at 8:30 P.M., as a one-hour animated musical special on the NBC network. It was sponsored by Timex. Like that company's watches, which "take a lickin' and keep on tickin'," *Magoo*'s ratings were so good that the network repeated its broadcast during the Christmas season of 1963 and for several subsequent Yuletide showings.

Viewers lucky enough to catch the program knew why. *Mister Magoo's Christmas Carol* was a genuinely first-rate adaptation, sweet, gripping, tuneful, and tender. Not to mention unique. For if one examines the varying versions of *A*

Christmas Carol gathered in this book, it quickly becomes apparent that the best adaptations have primarily been live-action ones.

How surprising, then, that one of the best animated *Carols* is also the best *musical* version. Plus one of the most downright enjoyable, surprisingly moving, and finest all-round adaptations ever made.

And how ironic that it should star a bald, nearsighted, crotchety cartoon character.

The myopic hero of *Mr. Magoo's Christmas Carol* first came upon the scene in the late 1940s through the efforts of UPA (United Productions of America), an organization founded in 1943 by a group of young animators who'd broken away from the Walt Disney Company two years before, after an artist's strike. Known for its imaginative, then-radical cartoon design, which ignored standard animation to concentrate on a simpler yet more stylized technique, UPA employed an honored roster of artists like Stephen Bosustow (a founder of the company), John Hubley, and Ernest Pintoff. These men and a few others were responsible for nearly two decades' worth of sophisticated product.

Among UPA's better-known achievements are an animated adaptation of James Thurber's *Unicorn in the Garden* and the creation of delightfully original characters like *Gerald McBoing Boing*, a little boy who could only talk in bizarre sound effects.

However, UPA's most famous and popular invention was Mr. Magoo. A

Magoo utters Scrooge's most famous line.

short, irascible, incredibly nearsighted character whose bad vision caused endless complications, Magoo first appeared in the 1949 UPA cartoon *Ragtime Bear*. His trademark mannerisms were inspired by the personality of W. C. Fields—plus a stubborn old uncle of UPA artist John Hubley.

But most viewers would probably agree that the man who *really* brought Mr. Magoo to life was the man who did his voice: Jim Backus.

Backus was an actor-comedian who delivered Magoo's dialogue in every *Mr. Magoo* cartoon, feature-length film, and network television show. Known as one of the most genuinely funny men and best raconteurs in the business, Backus was born February 25, 1913, in Cleveland; he died July 13, 1989, after a ten-year illness complicated by Parkinson's disease.

A failed stage actor, Jim Backus first achieved success as a comical, unbelievably rich snob named Hubert Updyke, who was a recurring radio character on *The Alan Young Show* in the 1940s. Later Backus moved into television, first as the cohost of a variety show called *Hollywood House*, then as Joan Davis's harassed but loving husband on *I Married Joan*. Though he also did extensive film work (with his best-known performance being the henpecked father of James Dean in *Rebel Without a Cause*), Backus is today primarily remembered for his TV role as marooned millionaire Thurston Howell III on *Gilligan's Island*.

In his 1965 autobiography *Only When I Laugh*, Backus recalled how he would frequently ad-lib Magoo's dialogue. Actually, this was a chancy procedure,

Jim Backus and myopic alter ego Mr. Magoo.

since cartoon characters have their lip movements synced to their words *after* their human counterparts have recorded the lines. But Backus's growling, muttering ad-libs were often so much better than Magoo's scripted salvos that these improvised asides surely helped the cartoon character sustain his twenty-five-plus year career.

That career included many UPA shorts. Among the best of these are *Captain's Outrageous* (1952), *When Magoo Flew* (1954, shot in Cinemascope), and *Magoo's Puddle Jumper* (1956). Those last two, incidentally, won Academy Awards. The high ratings of *Magoo's Carol* also prompted NBC to give the character his own primetime 1964–65 television series. This was titled *The Famous Adventures of Mr. Magoo*; in it, Magoo portrayed historical figures like Rip Van Winkle and King Arthur. Magoo later popped up on *What's New, Mr. Magoo?*, a 1977 CBS Saturday morning cartoon show.

Interestingly, although many animation buffs are quite familiar with Mr. Magoo's appearance in his hour-long *Christmas Carol*, what's not quite so well known is the fact that Magoo also starred in a number of *feature-length*, UPA-produced animated films. Most of these were released in the early-to-mid sixties, with the exception of *1001 Arabian Nights* (1959), which was later televised as a feature-length special. Other Magoo features had titles like *Mr. Magoo in Sherwood Forest* (1964), *Mr. Magoo: Man of Mystery* (also 1964), *Mr. Magoo in the King's Service* (1966), and *Mr. Magoo's Little Snow White* (released theatrically on a double bill in 1970, along with *Magoo's Carol*!).

The Spirit of Christmas Past helps Scrooge fly back to his boyhood.

The Cratchit family, UPA style.

But despite Magoo's long and honorable history, the character's shining hour was *Mr. Magoo's Christmas Carol*. Here's why:

⊛ Magoo was the ideal substitute for Scrooge in this film, since the nearsighted character's already-curmudgeonly nature perfectly fit Ebenezer's own sour personality.

⊛ Jim Backus, perhaps realizing that he'd been given a rare chance to play Magoo for something other than laughs, seized the opportunity by delivering a dramatic vocal performance that more than matches the film's (surprisingly straight) retelling of Dickens's narrative.

⊛ There are in-jokes. Tiny Tim is played by Gerald McBoing Boing, who not only talks, but sings!

⊛ Numerous creative touches demonstrate the innovative flair which made UPA famous. For example, the plot concerns Mr. Magoo starring in a Broadway musical adaptation of *A Christmas Carol*. And the action is staged as a play-within-a-film. The start of each "act" is signaled by a point-of-view shot of the camera sitting in the auditorium with the play's audience. Then the curtains rise, the camera pushes forward, and we're back into the story.

⊛ Additionally, for a cartoon starring a notably comic character, *Mr. Magoo's*

Christmas Carol is an unexpectedly *restrained* piece of work. Nowhere is this subdued approach more apparent than in the film's treatment of Magoo's myopia. Though the character's bad vision always results in disastrous consequences, these calamities only occur during the beginning and the end of *Mr. Magoo's Christmas Carol*. Which leaves the central narrative untouched, and allows viewers to follow Barbara Chain's tight, faithful script without being distracted by a lot of unnecessary *shtick*.

At this point Ye Author could continue by noting a number of other worthwhile elements in *Mr. Magoo's Christmas Carol*. Such as the superior vocal performances by the film's supporting cast: Jack Cassidy (Cratchit), Royal Dano (Marley's Ghost), Jane Keen (Belle Fezziwig), Les Tremayne (Christmas Present), Joan Gardner (Tiny Tim and Christmas Past), Morey Amsterdam (several characters), and Paul Frees (who gave voice to at least three different characters). Or the surprising depths of emotion director Abe Levitow brought to *Magoo's* "Christmas Past" sequences. Or how wonderfully absorbing, atmospheric, and heartfelt the entire production is.

But the heck with all that; what everyone *really* loves about this adaptation is its music.

Mr. Magoo's Christmas Carol is brimming with absolutely magnificent melodies. And unlike most other musical *Carols*, you *will* be humming these

A rare one-sheet showing the 1970 theatrical release of the made-for-TV Mr. Magoo's Christmas Carol, *double-billed with the feature-length* Mr. Magoo's Little Snow White.

"Autographed" give-away to patrons of the 1970 theatrical release of Mr. Magoo's Christmas Carol.

tunes as you're rewinding the *Magoo* tape (which is available from Paramount Home Video). *Every song* is a winner.

The music for *Magoo's* Broadway-like show tunes (another fitting UPA touch) was composed by the legendary Jule Styne. Born in 1905, in London, Styne (real name Jules Stein) began his musical career at the age of eight as a concert pianist. He then was a bandleader and a vocal arranger before moving to Hollywood in the mid-1930s, where he worked as a voice coach for screen legends like Shirley Temple.

Styne started composing for films in 1938. He had fruitful collaborations with other notable musical figures (Stephen Sondheim, Frank Loesser, Sammy Cahn, etc.) and ultimately wrote popular songs, Tin Pan Alley tunes, and numerous scores for film, television, and Broadway. In 1954, Styne won an Academy Award (with collaborator Sammy Cahn) for the title song of the film *Three Coins in the Fountain*. He also cowrote scores for *Gentleman Prefer Blondes* (1953), *Gypsy* (1963), and *Funny Girl* (1968).

For *Mr. Magoo's Christmas Carol*, Jule Styne wrote the music, while Bob Merrill (who wrote *Funny Girl* and others with Styne) did the lyrics. The highlights of their *Christmas Carol* score are:

Magoo enthusiastically proclaiming the joys of money ("Ringle, Ringle, Coins as They Jingle") while Bob Cratchit counterpoints him with complaints about the temperature ("It's Cold, It's Cold, It's Cold!"); the heartrendingly sad "All Alone

in the World" (sung when Magoo has been abandoned as a child on Christmas Eve); "Razzleberry Dressing," the amusing Cratchit dinner tune, which celebrates that unusual side dish as well as deserts like "Woofeljelly Cake."

In fact, there's only one less-than-perfect tune here. That's "Winter Was Warm," which is sung by Scrooge's fiancée before she breaks her engagement. And its primary fault is that, in a score full-to-bursting with excellent songs, "Winter" is merely *good*.

Sadly, the wonderful music found in *Mister Magoo's Christmas Carol* is not currently available on cassette or compact disc. What a shame; to paraphrase Leonard Maltin's comment about the year-round appropriateness of the Alastair Sim *Carol*, *Mr. Magoo's* soundtrack is far too good to be heard only at Christmas time.

And that's the *only* negative comment Ye Author has to make about this otherwise outstanding offering.

Mr. Magoo's Christmas Carol is a terrific family film in the best meaning of that phrase: charming, touching, and eminently entertaining. Suitable for adults and children alike, this is definitely one videotape anyone would be overjoyed to find under the tree come Christmas morning.

Right next to a bowlful of razzleberry dressing, of course!

TRIVIA QUESTIONS
(Answers on page 226)

Mr. Magoo's Christmas Carol

1. Name the animator who created Mr. Magoo.

2. Name the two composers responsible for the fine songs in *Mr. Magoo's Christmas Carol*.

3. At the beginning of *Magoo's Carol*, we see a montage of bright city lights, neon signs, and spinning newspaper headlines. Name the *Variety*-like newspaper in this scene that bears the headline, "Critics Laud Magoo's Carol."

4. Does Magoo arrive at the theater on time for his performance of *A Christmas Carol*?

5. Of course, most of us know that Jim Backus was the voice of Mr. Magoo. However, can you also give the title of a film in which Backus wore an apron? And what's the *full* name of the character he played on *Gilligan's Island*?

6. Where do we first see Magoo singing the song "Ringle, Ringle, Coins When They Jingle"? What's he doing as he sings?

7. After Magoo sees Marley's face superimposed on his doorknocker, what does he

do and what does he say? (HINT: Magoo's dialogue refers to eyes.)

8. When Marley's Ghost first appears, unlike other Scrooges, Magoo does *not* initially blame the sight of this apparition on "an undigested bit of beef" or "a fragment of an underdone potato." On what foodstuff *does* Magoo blame the vision of Marley's Ghost?

9. Time to compare this question with the response found in other versions of *A Christmas Carol*—at what time does Marley's Ghost appear to Magoo?

10. The biggest difference between this version of the Dickens tale and all other ones has something to do with the three Ghosts of Christmas. In fact, it's such a difference that virtually no other version has it. Can you spot it?

11. What famous UPA cartoon character plays Tiny Tim? What does that character do here he hardly ever does in any other film appearance?

12. What is Tiny Tim's favorite food? His second favorite?

13. Can you sing the chorus—or at least recite the words—to "All Alone in the World"? At what point in *Magoo's Carol* do we first hear this melancholy song?

14. What does the Ghost of Christmas Past carry in its right hand?

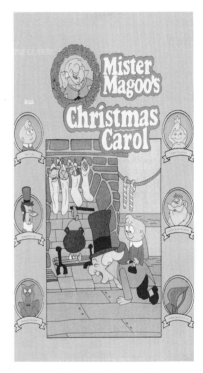

Paramount Home Video box art: Mr. Magoo's Christmas Carol.

15. How does the Ghost of Christmas Past know its time grows short?

16. What is the Ghost of Christmas Yet-to-Come called in this version? What does it look like? Do you ever see its face?

17. What are the names of the three businessman laughing about Scrooge's death, the ones Magoo listens to in the Future?

18. What personal objects does the undertaker take from Magoo's dead body? Where does he sell them?

19. How many Cratchit children are there?

20. Who plays Scrooge's nephew Fred in this version?

21. What is the address of the Cratchit home in this version?

22. Where is Magoo the second time he sings "All Alone in the World"?

23. At story's end, what's on the top of the Cratchit's Christmas tree?

24. Although *Magoo's Carol* was specifically made for television, it was also released theatrically as part of a double bill. Name the year this happened, as well as the name of the cofeature with which it played.

25. What is Mr. Magoo's last line?

CHAPTER ELEVEN
THE BEST
ANIMATED VERSION

A CHRISTMAS CAROL
(USA/GREAT BRITAIN, 1971) RATING: ★★★

The 1971 *Carol* is the most successful attempt to render a purely *artistic* vision of a Dickens tale ever put on film. That it's in the animated format is a marvelous bonus.

Why? Because when most Americans hear the word "animation," they immediately think of tedious kiddie-oriented cartoon shows. With good reason; for the past thirty years, American audiences have been spoonfed a never-ending diet of insipid animated product, pablum specifically aimed at the lowest common denominator. Anyone seeking verification of this mass-market attitude need simply switch on a TV set to any Saturday morning cartoon show.

Yet the art of animation doesn't only traffic in the dull, the simplistic, or the obvious. Many serious, resolutely *adult* animated films have been produced as well. Usually by independent filmmakers, unhampered by the strict commercial guidelines laid down by such "cartoon factories" as Disney or Hanna-Barbera. Most of these works are usually short films, too, since feature-length cartoons demand inordinate amounts of time and money, bankrupting investments far beyond the reach of most independents.

So while they may not get as much exposure as the ordinary garden-variety cartoon, mature animated works by talented filmmakers from Canada, England, America, Russia, Japan, Eastern Europe—indeed, from the entire globe—have been produced for as long as there have been animation stands.

As for the best animated *Christmas Carol*, this first premiered on the night of December 21, 1971, as a special ABC holiday presentation. Its running time was a scant twenty-six minutes. Yet from its opening shot of grimy factory chimneys belching black smoke into a sooty London sky, to its closing moments of an old miser's spiritual conversion, this imaginative, handsomely wrought production consistently revealed itself to be one of the most creative and painstakingly authentic adaptations of Dickens's work.

This faithfulness was no accident. The 1971 *Carol* was primarily created by two giants of animation—Chuck Jones and Richard Williams. And according to a 1977 interview in *Film News*, Jones (who was the 1971 version's executive produc-

Executive Producer Chuck Jones (right) and producer/director Richard Williams (center) confer with a technician on how best to animate a cel of artwork for A Christmas Carol.

er) insisted that his *Christmas Carol* took even its stage directions directly from Dickens's book.

"Dickens tells you exactly where the stove is and the chair," Jones explained, "and where the window is in relation to the fireplace. And when Marley shows up, you don't have to wonder which way Scrooge turns his head, because it's right there in Dickens. There is a also a very careful description of Bob Cratchit. Usually, he's portrayed as pinched and bent over and afraid to relax. Dickens shows him with a ramrod up his back. It's Marley and Scrooge who are actually bent over."

The name Chuck Jones should ring as many bells to animation fans as are rung throughout London on Christmas morning. A multiple Oscar winning producer and director, Charles M. Jones was born on September 1, 1912, in Spokane, Washington. He entered the cartoon business in the 1930s, as an assembly-line cartoonist for such well-known animators as Ub Iwerks and Walter Lantz. Jones later joined the Warner Brothers cartoon unit, where he created the famous Road Runner character (*Beep beep!*) and helped co-create the even more well-known Bugs Bunny, Daffy Duck, Porky Pig, Tweetie Pie, and Sylvester the Cat. After leaving Warners in the early sixties, Jones joined MGM, before moving on to produce or direct such memorable shorts as *The Dot and the Line* and *Horton Hears a Who* and the full-length *Phantom Tollbooth*.

At the time of Jones's involvement with *A Christmas Carol*, he was an

Scrooge (the voice of Alastair Sim) is shocked to see his doorknocker transform into the head of his dead partner.

administrative vice-president for ABC Television and the head of a separate production division dubbed "ABC's Curiosity Shop." It was in this capacity that Jones decided to create an animated *Carol*; he also decided to hand over the film's line-producing and directing chores to a remarkable British talent named Richard Williams.

"[Richard's] the only 'genius' genius to come along in animation in years," Jones told the *Los Angeles TV Times* in 1971. "He's only thirty-eight, which is still young according to our standards. But he is very precise, draws beautifully and is probably one of the most respected craftsman in the world."

High praise indeed, from an artist of Chuck Jones's caliber!

Richard Williams was born in 1933. A Canadian, he first began doing animation at the age of twelve. After briefly working for both Disney and UPA in the late 1940s, Williams then emigrated to England in 1955. His first directorial effort there, the thirty-minute symbolic short *The Little Island* (1958), brought him great acclaim.

Williams then branched out into television commercials, full-length animated films like *Raggedy Ann and Andy* (1977), and live-action features, for which he mostly contributed cleverly animated title sequences. Some of these latter assignments included the titles for *What's New, Pussycat?*, *Casino Royale*, *The Eliminator*, and *A Funny Thing Happened on the Way to the Forum*.

Richard Williams's best-known work, however, is certainly the animation he oversaw for the Disney Studio's mind-boggling *Who Killed Roger Rabbit*. A combination cartoon/live-action *film noir, Rabbit* found Williams responsible for directing the animation seen in that 1988 blockbuster. And for his efforts, Richard Williams received a special Academy Award for his groundbreaking work on the picture.

But what caused Chuck Jones to hire Williams to oversee *A Christmas Carol*? The answer lies in this 1971 quote Jones gave to the *Los Angeles Herald Examiner*:

"I was most impressed by Williams's animated work on the live-action 1968 British film, *The Charge of the Light Brigade*. Richard created both the title and some bridging sequences for that film, and achieved a special feeling by using animated copies of Victorian steel engraving techniques.

"Let me explain a bit farther," Jones continued. "Dickens was known as 'Boz.' That was his pen name. And although an artist named Leech illustrated the first edition of *A Christmas Carol*, the illustrator Dickens usually worked with signed his name 'Phiz' . . . and Phiz was really Hablot Knight Browne.

"Now, Browne's drawings were done with a steel engraving technique. The exact same style Richard had copied in *Charge*. Browne's engravings were rich in detail, and coincided in a very charismatic way with the flavor of the Christmas

Marley's ghost unwinds the bandage around its head with horrifying results.

story. Since our *Christmas Carol* animation [was going to be] based on those original drawings, and since Richard had already demonstrated a fluency with the technique needed to achieve those drawings—well, this just seemed like one of those marriages made in heaven. And it was. Richard's steel engravings for *A Christmas Carol* [were] wonderful."

At the time Richard Williams was contacted by Chuck Jones to creatively helm *A Christmas Carol*, the Canadian animator was working out of his own studio, based in London's Soho Square. Happily, Williams agreed with Jones that their *Carol* should be completely faithful to its source material.

"We are doing this show as Dickens would do it if he were the producer," Williams commented at the time of production.

To achieve an authenticity beyond the mere text found in Dickens's story, Jones and Williams initially utilized the John Leech, first-edition *Christmas Carol* illustrations as visual inspiration for their own *Carol*'s "look." Richard Williams also spent two weeks in the archives of the British Museum, poring over the original "Phiz" drawings.

But it was more than old illustrations that influenced Williams's work. Animators from his studio were sent to Dickens's home at Gad's Hill for further visual inspiration. It was in Dickens's own house that the researchers made countless pencil sketches of his library, furniture, and other artifacts, to use as later reference points.

Scrooge recoils in terror from the Spirits of Ignorance and Want, revealed to be hiding beneath Christmas Present's robe.

Two other *Christmas Carol* animators working on Williams's team also did exhaustive research in the British Museum, meticulously examining every visual remnant they could find relating to 1843 London. "They researched everything," Jones enthused. "Even doorknobs. The scrollwork and details of buildings were also copied."

After this intensive archaeology was concluded, Williams and his animating team (which included four American animators Jones had sent to London from Los Angeles), turned to the actual task of producing a short cartoon version of *A Christmas Carol* itself. This process took nine months and over 30,000 individual drawings, or "cels," to complete. By contrast, the average half-hour Saturday morning cartoon utilizes only three thousand cels.

In order to bring movement to *A Christmas Carol*, each separate drawing was done directly on a sheet of clear plastic acetate, after which the color was laid in. This resulted in individual pictures with a great deal of surface texture, subtle detailing that added one more layer of artistic enhancement to the film.

Each series of pictures relating to one particular moment in the film—say a shot of Scrooge frowning—would then be physically fastened together in the proper order in a long belt (or "run") of cels. These would pass beneath the animation camera on a picture-by-picture basis.

The end result?

Fluid, believable movement.

But completing the film's animation was only half the job; music and

human voices were needed as well. To this end Tristram Cary, son of the English novelist Joyce Cary, and a film/television composer who'd previously scored classic English films like *Five Million Years to Earth*, was hired to both compose the music for the Jones/Williams film and to direct the Sinfonia of London for *A Christmas Carol*'s soundtrack.

Then there were the human actors who would give the cartoon characters voice. First the distinguished British thespian Sir Michael Redgrave was signed on to narrate the film, using Dickens's own prose; Redgrave also verbally "bridged" some of the story sequences. And in a nod to the excellent 1951 live-action version, Michael Hordern was persuaded to vocally reprise his role as Marley's Ghost.

The excellence of the 1951 *Carol* also prompted Jones and Williams to choose the one actor–the *only* actor–both men felt should supply the voice of Scrooge.

Alastair Sim.

Having already put his unique stamp on the famous miser in the 1951 version, however, Sim was initially reluctant to accept the animators' offer.

"We were told that the idea of getting Alastair Sim for Scrooge was out of the question," Jones related to the *Los Angeles TV Times* in 1971. "But eventually, Sim was convinced to do it. Solely on the 'Dickens dedication' that went into [our show]. Even though he'd already appeared in such an acclaimed adaptation, Sim felt that [our effort] was the *definitive* version of *A Christmas Carol*. And if he did

this one, there would never be any reason to play it again."

Sim's vocal performance throughout the 1971 *Carol* can't be faulted. Once again, this fine character actor imbued Scrooge with the varying shades of miserliness and repentance so vital to the character's believability. The participation of Sim also lent a note of poignancy; twenty years after he'd last *pretended* to be an aged miser, the cracked, quavering voice of Alastair Sim in 1971 revealed that he had, in actuality, finally become an old man.

The total cost for the Jones/Williams *Christmas Carol* was $300,000. Which, in 1971 dollars, was approximately five times the budget of an average half-hour Saturday morning cartoon show. But enough production details—how does the 1971 production play?

In a word, wonderfully.

The most striking thing about the animated 1971 *Carol* is how dynamically *cinematic* it is. For instance, after the opening credits, the first sequence is a dizzying, gravity-defying overhead tracking shot, looking down onto the city of London. The camera almost seems to be in free-fall as it rakes across the tops of buildings and numerous facades, before finally coming to rest on the lighted windows of Scrooge's office.

The 1971 *Carol* also offers startling, nearly surreal brush strokes. For example, the Ghost of Christmas Past is not only meticulously recreated as Dickens described it—as a pale, young/old figure with a flame jetting from its head—but

The Ghost of Christmas Yet-to-Come points out a certain tombstone to Scrooge.

Richard Williams makes it waver in and out of focus; he double and triple exposes the figure as well. The end result is a Past Ghost with *multiple heads and eight eyes*, a bizarre, nightmarish apparition which could easily have sprung from the canvas of a Dali or Picasso.

Even more impressive are Williams's deft manipulations of time and space. Through the limitless expression which only animation can achieve, backgrounds shift and mutate in the twinkling of an eye. Rapid-fire montages suggest the flow of time. And when Scrooge is taken to his childhood by the Ghost of Christmas Past, only the sound of his frightened heartbeat accompanies Ebenezer's vertiginous flight above a disorienting jumble of London rooftops.

"Dick [Williams] also did something, in the Christmas Present section, that has never been done before," Chuck Jones went on to the *Los Angeles TV Times*. "First, he worked with Dickens's idea that Christmas is at home not only in London, but everywhere, all around the world. And *simultaneously*—which is little more than a single sentence in the original book. But Dick felt it was important to tell it graphically.

"So there is a sequence in which Scrooge and the Ghost of Christmas Present fly all around the world. It only runs about fifteen seconds . . . but it took over a month to animate that one scene alone."

Jones is not quite correct in claiming that a sequence of Ebenezer watching Christmas being celebrated in other parts of the world is totally unique to his

Cityscape detail from A Christmas Carol *and an excellent example of director Richard Williams's "steel-engraving" technique.*

Christmas Carol. For example, the Alastair Sim version has the Ghost of Christmas Present take Scrooge to a tiny town of coal miners, "who labor in the bowels of the earth." And there are a few other adaptations which also take Scrooge away from his native London (versions which Ye Author insists you track down yourself, since they *are* all listed in this book!).

However, Jones is correct in one sense; no other *Christmas Carol* has so perfectly captured the worldwide significance of the Christmas spirit, in a single scene, as does this version.

In quick order, the 1971 Scrooge witnesses the holiday festivities occurring within the dim, dark home of a family of poor miners (in one of the film's most gorgeously "lit" moments); sees the celebrations of two isolated lighthouse keepers; hears the sound of a Christmas hymn being sung by a solitary sailor, as he pilots his ship through dark winter seas.

Yet the 1971 *Christmas Carol* is not only about stunning cinematic technique, for Jones and Williams took great pains to evoke the melancholy of Dickens's fable as well. We see darkness, rats, and smoke; become enveloped in a thick, featureless fog, whose sole illumination is a distant burning lamp; watch a sobbing Bob Cratchit grieving over the bed-sheeted body of a dead Tiny Tim; are made to experience a genuine feeling of dread at the frightening appearance of Marley's eerie ghost.

Williams and Jones are on record as having thought that their *Christmas*

Carol was a new, true "first edition" of Dickens's story. Ye Author wholeheartedly agrees. However, I also should point out that I do have one (and only one) rather strong complaint about this 1971 adaptation:

It's too *short*.

"Dickens was apparently not informed that TV shows [can only] run twenty-six minutes," Chuck Jones said, "so we did have to cut a bit. If you [did] it exactly as Dickens wrote it, it [would have run] thirty-three minutes. We couldn't pad that to an hour, so we had no choice but to cut to twenty-six minutes. But that's good, because ours is probably the least padded of all versions."

Also a most satisfying—if necessarily condensed—animated version of Dickens's perennial classic, one which has the distinction of being the only *Christmas Carol* to win an Academy Award.

For Best Short Subject, Animated Film, in 1972.

TRIVIA QUESTIONS
(Answers on page 228)

A Christmas Carol (1971)

1. At what time does this particular version of *A Christmas Carol* begin?

2. What's the original shape of the knocker on Scrooge's front door? The one that

changes into the face of Jacob Marley.

3. When Scrooge comes home from work, what passes him on his dark staircase?

4. How does Marley's Ghost convince Scrooge he's a genuine phantom?

5. Name all the pieces of furniture in Scrooge's living room.

6. After Marley's Ghost leaves through Scrooge's window, what does Ebenezer see in the outside world?

7. How does the Fezziwig of Richard Williams's *Carol* celebrate Christmas?

8. What's unusual about the Ghost of Christmas Past (other than the fact that it's a ghost, of course)?

9. What other well-known animated Christmas film did Chuck Jones *direct*? And on what cartoon did Jones receive his first directorial credit?

10. What does the Ghost of Christmas Past hold in its right hand? Its left? What does Scrooge do with that thing in the Spirit's left hand?

11. What does Tiny Tim have on his left leg?

12. Everyone expects the Ghost of Christmas present to show Scrooge the Cratchit's Christmas dinner and Scrooge's nephew Fred's Christmas party. But name two *other* holiday scenes this Spirit reveals to Scrooge.

13. How many separate drawings did it take to make this film?

14. What is the sex of the Spirits of Ignorance and Want?

15. At what time does the Ghost of Christmas Yet-to-Come arrive for Scrooge?

16. What color are Scrooge's eyes?

17. When Scrooge, accompanied by the Ghost of Christmas Yet-to-Come, witnesses a group of former business acquaintances discussing Ebenezer's funeral, by what nickname do they refer to Scrooge?

18. What's unusual about the sign advertising the "Prize Turkey" in the butcher's shop near the end of the film?

19. As is consistent with many other versions, Bob Cratchit arrives late for work the day after Christmas. But at what *time* does he arrive in this version? And how does his lateness relate to the only continuity error in the film?

20. Which is the only version of *A Christmas Carol* to win an Academy Award?

CHAPTER TWELVE
THE DISNEY VERSION

MICKEY'S CHRISTMAS CAROL
(USA,1983) RATING: ★★★

Given the many animated films based on classic books produced by the Walt Disney studio over the years, it's puzzling that it took them so long to adapt a venerable fantasy like *A Christmas Carol.*

Just as it's a disappointment that when Disney finally got around to it, such a routine product was produced.

Then again, maybe the ho-hum quality of *Mickey's Carol* is forgivable. At least in the historical sense. For this animated short was released during a decline in Disney's corporate fortunes; the company showed a definite lack of direction following the 1966 death of founder Walt Disney, and *Mickey's Carol* was produced at the tail-end of that downward spiral, only a few years before the new management team of Jefferey Katzenberg and Michael Eisner would revitalize the studio with

smash hits like *The Little Mermaid, Beauty and the Beast, Aladdin,* and *The Lion King.*

Unfortunately, timing is everything. And *Mickey's Carol* seems to have suffered because of that.

But let's take the positive side first. *Mickey's Christmas Carol* is a pleasant, fitfully amusing, straightforward adaptation of Dickens's story. One that's been slightly reworked so that Ebenezer Scrooge is now played by Scrooge McDuck. An avaricious, penny-pinching character (with a Scottish accent) who was just as miserly when originally created by writer-artist Carl Barks as he is here playing Ebenezer Scrooge.

Another plus to *Mickey's Carol* is the vocal presence of the gentle, quietly intelligent actor who did Scrooge McDuck's voice; Alan Young. Born November 19, 1919 in North Shields, Northumberland, England, Young started his career as a teenager in Canadian radio. He worked in American radio beginning in the mid-forties and, by the end of that decade, was quite popular. This fame landed him a job in the then-fledgling medium of television as the star of *The Alan Young Show,* a moderately successful variety program which ran from 1950 through 1953. He subsequently made guest appearances on a number of other TV shows before (reluctantly) agreeing to play straight man to a talking horse on the amazingly popular *Mr. Ed,* a 1961–66 show whose bouncy theme song has remained stubbornly embedded in the subconscious of an entire generation of baby boomers.

The ghost of Jacob Marley (Goofy) visits Ebenezer Scrooge (Scrooge McDuck). © Walt Disney Productions

Young went into semi-retirement in the late 1960s to devote his life to Christian Science. He then returned to TV in the mid-seventies for occasional guest appearances on programs like *The Love Boat*, or to do voiceovers for Saturday morning cartoon shows like *The Smurfs*. Since then he has been little-seen, and much missed.

As for the animation in *Mickey's Christmas Carol*, it's fluid and professional. Also uninspired; this version is hardly in the same league with the Richard Williams version. Still, children should enjoy the cameo appearances by the many famous Disney characters who pop up in this film.

Oddly, the most famous Disney character of them all has the smallest part—Mickey himself, playing the role of Bob Cratchit (but still acting like Mickey). The Mouse is relegated to a bit part that's not much more than a glorified walk-on. Mickey only appears in a few scenes, which suggests that this effort could have been more truthfully titled "Scrooge McDuck's Christmas Carol."

But look at *Mickey's* supporting cast! Cartoon historians will love the fact that so many well-known Disney characters appear on the same program. Jiminy Cricket (from *Pinocchio*) is the Ghost of Christmas Past, Goofy plays Marley's Ghost, Daisy Duck is Scrooge's spurned fiancée, Mr. Toad portrays Fezziwig, Donald Duck is Scrooge's nephew Fred—the list goes on and on. In fact, part of the fun here is trying to guess which famous cartoon character will appear next.

On the negative side, *Mickey's Christmas Carol* has no real heart or soul.

This is strictly a factory job—well made, certainly, but flavorless. There's also an overreliance on stale, silly humor, not the best idea for a cartoon that's mostly played for laughs (for instance, when Goofy shows up as Marley's Ghost, he immediately trips over his chains).

So let's call *Mickey's Christmas Carol* "Dickens Lite." There *is* one scene that jumpstarts the story—the Ghost of Christmas Yet-to-Come kicks Scrooge into his grave, and the screaming duck plummets toward a seething caldron of fire. But for the most part, this is an uninspired, by-the-numbers adaptation with little wit or imagination. *Mickey's Carol* will best serve as an animated baby-sitter for toddlers enchanted by the Magic of the Mouse.

As Ye Author has written elsewhere in this book, parents who really *care* about their kids will show them the Richard Williams or Mr. Magoo adaptations instead.

One important footnote to this Disney film has little to do with *Mickey's Christmas Carol* itself (well, alright, maybe more than a little). This is the fact that, although *Mickey's Carol* is now in release by Disney as a stand-alone cassette titled "Walt Disney's Mini-Classics," the *first* video release of this picture (which occurred on the "Walt Disney Home Video" label in 1984), also contained an interesting documentary on the *making* of *Mickey's Christmas Carol*.

It's this 1984 cassette that cartoon connoisseurs will want to seek out. The reason? Because "The Making of *Mickey's Christmas Carol*"—a twenty-four-minute,

shot-on-video documentary—is actually better than the main feature itself.

Not by much, though. The *Making of* documentary gives off an irritating, self-congratulatory tone which tries to convince us that *Mickey's Christmas Carol* is some sort of modern classic. It isn't. There's also a distressing lack of hard information about its genesis. Nowhere in the documentary, for example, is it mentioned that this adaptation originally started out as a *musical*. Or that all the songs (save a saccharine melody titled "Oh, What a Merry Christmas Day," sung over the opening credits), were subsequently cut out of the short before this cartoon's release.

"The Making of *Mickey's Christmas Carol*," however, really shines in its historical overviews of a few Disney characters. Numerous clips of old cartoons featuring Mickey Mouse, Donald Duck, and other well-known critters are included, as well as a fascinating, if brief, retrospective on how The Mouse has changed his "look" over the years. There's also a smattering of interesting information—Donald Duck's first cartoon appearance, for instance, was in *The Little Hen* (1934).

The Cratchit family, Disney style. © Walt Disney Productions

Best of all are the short on-camera interviews with such legendary figures as Clarence "Ducky" Nash, Hal Smith, and Jimmy MacDonald. The same three men who, respectively, were the voices of Donald Duck, Goofy, and Mickey Mouse.

So track down the older, 1984 release of this tape. Once you've seen *Mickey's Christmas Carol* you'll then be able to scan an occasionally

effective documentary that examines the past history of the very characters you've just watched.

Having written that, Ye Author feels compelled to end this chapter with a request:

Hey there, Mr. Wildly Successful Walt Disney Studio:

Don't you think it's time to tackle a tad more *ambitious* adaptation of *A Christmas Carol*?

This time, you could even star The Mouse.

TRIVIA QUESTIONS
(Answers on page 229)

Mickey's Christmas Carol

1. Name a popular television program which starred the actor who supplied the voice of Scrooge McDuck (HINT: his costar was a talking animal). Name the man who supplied the *voice* of this talking animal. Now name a classic *fantasy* film in which the English-born actor who supplied the voice of Scrooge McDuck portrayed a red-haired Scotsman–plus his own son!

2. What's unusual about the sign hanging over Scrooge McDuck's office door? The one that reads "Scrooge and Marley"?

Ebenezer Scrooge confronts the Ghost of Christmas Yet-to-Come (Black Pete) in Mickey's Christmas Carol *(1983). © Walt Disney Productions*

3. In this version, Mickey Mouse (playing Bob Cratchit) *doesn't* want to put an extra coal on the fire to keep warm. Why *does* he need that extra coal?

4. What year was Mickey Mouse first seen on the screen? What was the name of that cartoon?

5. Until 1984, three different people supplied the voice of Mickey Mouse. Who were they?

6. What rather cannibalistic dinner does Scrooge's nephew Fred (Donald Duck) plan on having for Christmas?

7. What present does Fred give to Scrooge McDuck?

8. Who, at least until 1984, had always supplied the voice of Donald Duck? In what year did Donald first appear on the screen? In what cartoon?

9. Who was the producer-director of *Mickey's Christmas Carol*? Where, how, and when did he get his start in the film business?

10. A sign is hanging on Scrooge McDuck's office wall. What does it say?

11. What does Scrooge McDuck do to his doorknocker immediately after it changes into the face of Marley?

Ebenezer Scrooge joins the Cratchit fun. © *Walt Disney Productions*

145

12. What does the gold badge on the inside of Jiminy Cricket's coat say?

13. How many Mickey Mouse cartoons had been made through 1983?

14. Who portrays Fezziwig? What musical instrument does he play?

15. Who plays Isabel, young Scrooge McDuck's lost love?

16. Daisy Duck wasn't always called that. What was this feminine fowl's name at the beginning of her cartoon career?

17. What does the Giant Ghost of Christmas Present use as a flashlight while walking through the streets of London?

18. Something's boiling in a pot on the hearth of Mickey's fireplace when Scrooge and the Giant spy on Bob Cratchit's home. What's inside that pot?

19. Name the Disney artist who animated both Mickey Mouse and Jiminy Cricket for this film.

20. What does the Ghost of Christmas Yet-to-Come look like? Does he speak? Name one thing he does which has never been done by any other version of this character.

21. On what previously released Disney project was the script for *Mickey's Christmas Carol* partially based? Who wrote that project?

CHAPTER THIRTEEN
OTHER ANIMATED VERSIONS

ALVIN'S CHRISTMAS CAROL
(USA, 1983) RATING: ★★

A half-hour episode from the Saturday morning children's cartoon show of the 1980s, *Alvin and the Chipmunks*, also available as a stand-alone cassette from Buena Vista Home Video.

In this limited-animation musical program, a brash chipmunk named Alvin is so obsessed about what presents he'll receive on Christmas Day that he forgets to buy gifts for his brothers Theodore and Simon, as well as for the kindly human ("Uncle Dave") under whose roof the three live. Several events then occur to snap Alvin out of his selfishness.

First, he thoughtlessly ruins the newspaper of an elderly neighbor by toss-

ing it into a birdbath. Next Alvin must compose an essay for school, titled "The True Meaning of Christmas." And while working on this homework assignment, he falls asleep, to dream of a visit by three Christmas Ghosts. They show Alvin that his thoughtlessness has caused that elderly neighbor great emotional pain; the lonely old man's only pleasure in life was his daily newspaper.

The plot synopsis for *Alvin's Christmas Carol* reveals that this story is aimed squarely at children. If taken as such, *Alvin* is an inoffensive morality tale that should amuse the kiddies. Although the screechy, chattering voices of the chipmunks themselves, *especially* their high-pitched singing, might make some adults run screaming out the room.

Alvin also teaches children a valuable lesson. In Uncle Dave's words, "There's more to Christmas than just getting presents. The holidays are a time of sharing, of giving to others."

Baby boomers might be interested to know that *Alvin's Christmas Carol* contains a rendition of "Christmas Don't Be Late," a novelty tune that topped the charts in the late 1950s. This particular song was the brainchild of Ross Bagdasarian, who, under the stage name David Seville, recorded that tune by using a speeded-up tape recording of his own voice (Bagdasarian used the same gimmick in 1958 for the equally popular novelty song "The Witch Doctor"). Bagdasarian then went on to visualize the personas of Alvin and his brothers for *The Alvin Show*, a 1961–62 primetime animated cartoon show for ABC.

Alvin the Chipmunk and his brothers Simon (center) and Theodore (right).

After Bagdasarian died in 1972, his son Ross Jr. used his own voice as the star(s) of another chipmunk show. This half-hour series debuted in 1983 on the NBC network and was called *Alvin and the Chipmunks*—the program on which *Alvin's Christmas Carol* first appeared.

BR'ER RABBIT'S CHRISTMAS CAROL

Beloved Uncle Remus characters Br'er Rabbit, Br'er Fox, and Br'er Bear act out an animated, Deep South version of the *Carol*. Since Ye Author hasn't seen this one (yet), he can't write anything else about it, or give any production credits. It is out there, though, on the *Saban* video label.

A CHRISTMAS CAROL (AUSTRALIA, 1969) ★★

A cheap-looking, bargain-basement, limited-animation musical that's one of the worst *Carols* in this book.

First broadcast as a one-hour special by CBS on December 13, 1970, this forty-seven-minute exercise in tedium, produced by Walter J. Hucker, is now distributed by Rhino Video. But it's not worth a rental. Although many of the situations and much of the dialogue are lifted directly from the original story, the handling of Dickens's material is dull

The Cratchit family, boredom style: from the tedious 1969 animated Christmas Carol.

and uninspired. Plus, the animation is minimal. The direction by Zoran Janjic and songs by Richard Bowder are bad, too.

In all fairness, however, Ye Author should point out that the 1969 animated *Carol* does have its moments. One is a running gag showing Scrooge unable to sneeze. As the Ghost of Christmas Present tells him, "You're too *mean* to give away a good sneeze!" Another nice detail is the gold coin Ebenezer keeps rubbing between his fingers; it's the first sovereign he ever made. There's also a bizarre moment when Scrooge passes an organ grinder and his monkey on the snowy London streets. This might seem logical to you, but all Ye Author can ask is, a *monkey*? In *London*? In *winter*?

The 1969 *Carol* ends, incidentally, with an off-key rendition of "Joy to the World"—an unintentionally appropriate comment on the film's artistic merits. Lethargic, tuneless, and forgettable, this adaptation wouldn't please the least discriminating child.

In other words, forget it.

Rhino Video has much better items in their catalog than this.

A CHRISTMAS CAROL (AUSTRALIA, 1982) ★★

A most unusual Marley's Ghost, from the 1969 animated Carol.

This seventy-two-minute animated version from Burbank Films of Sydney, Australia—which *isn't* a musical, thank goodness—is a mostly routine adaptation. It's

also a definite improvement over the sorry 1969 version (which CBS kept rebroad-casting every holiday season for over ten years!).

The 1982 *Carol* features improved animation, more background detail and cheerier colors than the blue/black tonalities found in the 1969 version. Faster paced, it's also faithful to its source material. And the characters have been drawn with a bit more imagination as well.

What's most interesting about this version, however, are the numerous fresh touches it inserts into the storyline, new bits of business which can be found in no other *Carol*.

For instance:

- Marley's Ghost has bushy black eyebrows and dark smudges under his eyes, making him look like a member of the rock band *Kiss*.

- The viewer is actually shown Marley's death. Scrooge's partner slumps over his workdesk and dies; his head then metamorphoses into a skull.

- When the boyhood Scrooge is seen daydreaming in his schoolroom, he conjures up the imagined form of a fez-wearing Egyptian named Ali Baba. This detail was in Dickens's original story, and can be found in no other *Carol* adaptation.

- No Tiny Tim has ever had such a big set of dreamy blue eyes, or talked in such a breathy little whisper, as this one.

- The Ghost of Christmas Present asks Scrooge if he's hungry while the two of them are standing outside the Cratchit home, watching the family prepare Christmas dinner. After Ebenezer replies "Yes," the Ghost magically materializes a dinner plate on which is a piece of toast and a cup of tea.

- The Ghost of Christmas Yet-to-Come takes Scrooge to the offices of Scrooge & Marley. Here Ebenezer watches a *new tenant*, who took over the building after Scrooge's death, make a generous donation to a Christmas charity.

- The Future Ghost also magically waves his hand over Scrooge's grave (which looks like a sarcophagus), and the lid floats off the tomb by itself.

- When Scrooge joins his nephew Fred for Christmas dinner, all the guests begin to sing "Hark, the Herald Angels Sing." But Scrooge doesn't know the words!

Despite these imaginative touches, however, the 1982 version ultimately turns out to be not much more than a generic *Christmas Carol*; the characters and mood are as two-dimensional as the animation. However, this *is* a painless (if mundane) way for younger children to experience their first exposure to Dickens's story.

JETSONS CHRISTMAS CAROL, A (USA, 1985) ★★★

The Jetsons first premiered in 1962 as a series of half-hour, primetime animated episodes on ABC, but lasted only one year, until 1963. Basically a sitcom set in the future, the series followed the sci-fi misadventures of a comical nuclear family. Their names? Well, as the show's theme song told us: "Meet George Jetson. Jane, his wife. Daughter Judy. His boy Elroy."

And so on and so forth.

What was most obvious about *The Jetsons* was how it attempted to duplicate the format of *The Flintstones*, being set in the future instead of the past. Both series were produced by William Hanna and Joseph Barbera, two animators who'd scored initial success with their excellent, MGM-produced series of *Tom and Jerry* cartoons, which were released in the forties and fifties. After creating dozens of these still-wonderful MGM shorts, the two then opened their own Hanna-Barbera Productions, an intimidatingly prolific cartoon factory which eventually flooded television airwaves with such limited-animation series as *Quick Draw McGraw*, *Huckleberry Hound*, *Yogi Bear*, and many others.

While it might be argued that the assembly-line methods of Hanna-Barbera tolled the death knell of quality animation, the company did manage to score its share of hits. One was *The Jetsons*, which today is something of a cult show. It's easy to see why: the program was littered with zany, attention-grabbing gadgets,

A good character shot of Scrooge from the otherwise dismal A Christmas Carol *(1969).*

high-tech machinery that included robot maids, pneumatic tubes that whisked people out of their cloud-scraping apartments, and ultra-quick ovens that cooked (and served) seven-course meals in under a minute.

Two made-for-TV *Jetson* movies were made in 1988—*Rockin' With Judy Jetson* and *The Flintstones Meet the Jetsons*—and there was a theatrical film, *The Jetsons—The Movie* in 1989. *The Jetsons* also returned to ABC as a new half-hour show, from 1985 to 1986. It's from that later network incarnation that *A Jetsons Christmas Carol* was drawn.

In this episode, Mr. Spacely, George's overbearing boss, forces Jetson to work on Christmas Eve. Meanwhile, after a holiday shopping spree at "The Moon Mall," the rest of the Jetsons return home to find that their dog has accidently swallowed part of a robot cat, which is causing the pooch severe gastrointestinal distress.

Mr. Spacely finally lets George leave work near midnight. Then, while counting his money, Spacely falls asleep and has a dream about being visited by his dead partner, who warns him that he will be visited by three Christmas Spirits. Two of these Spirits reveal that the Jetsons' dog has actually ingested a "Spacely Sprocket"—Spacely's prime product—and will soon die. Spacely's business empire will then

William Hanna (left) and Joseph Barbera surrounded by their creations for A Jetsons Christmas Carol.

be destroyed by a lawsuit the Jetsons bring against him.

A contrite Spacely awakens, hurries to the Jetsons' apartment with his personal veterinarian, and saves the dog. After distributing presents to the family, Spacely is then treated to the Jetsons singing "We Wish You a Merry Christmas," before hopping into his rocket car and zooming out of sight.

On one level, *A Jetsons Christmas Carol* is typical of the TV product ground out by the Hanna-Barbera studio; that is, there's an emphasis on juvenile humor and the expected gadgets. These include an automatic eggnog maker and a "Laser Tree" with orbiting Christmas ornaments.

Yet *A Jetsons Christmas Carol* isn't nearly the dopey experience one might expect. It moves quickly, features a fairly inventive script (by Marc Paykuss and Barbara Levy), and cleverly "futurizes" the basic *Christmas Carol* premise while still retaining the essence of the story.

The final verdict? Not bad. Rather cute, in fact.

A Jetsons Christmas Carol is available as a stand-alone cassette on the Hanna-Barbera Home Video label.

Alvin the Chipmunk receives a Christmas present from Uncle Dave's kindly grandmother.

STINGIEST MAN IN THE WORLD, THE (USA, 1978)

In 1978, a stop-motion, puppet animation *Carol* was shown on NBC; it was also a musical. Produced by Rankin-Bass, the same company which had had prior stop-

motion holiday hits with *Frosty the Snowman* and *Rudolph the Reindeer, The Stingiest Man in the World* featured the voice of Walter Matthau as Scrooge. As Ye Author must humbly confess to not having seen this version, no other details are available.

TRIVIA QUESTIONS

(Answers on page 231)

Alvin's Christmas Carol (1983)

1. Give the names of Alvin's chipmunk brothers.

2. Here's something different: at the beginning of the videotape containing *Alvin's Christmas Carol*, there's an advertisement (or "trailer") for *another* "Christmas Carol"—one that's discussed in this book! Can you name this other *Carol*?

3. Who created Alvin and the Chipmunks? Give both this person's stage name *and* his real name.

4. What is the name of Alvin's elderly neighbor? Also name that neighbor's cat.

5. What is Simon building in the basement as a present for Uncle Dave? What present is Theodore making?

6. Name the title of the homework assignment that Alvin must write about Christmas.

7. What is Alvin's full name?

A Christmas Carol (1969)

8. What supernatural event marks the arrival of Marley's Ghost? (HINT: It involves a bell.)

9. How does a local shopkeeper describe Scrooge's miserliness?

10. The physical appearance of Marley's Ghost is different here than in any other version. Describe it.

11. At what time does Marley say the Ghost of Christmas Yet-to-Come will appear?

12. The Ghost of Christmas Present notices that Scrooge is constantly rubbing a small object between his fingers. What is it?

A Christmas Carol (1982)

13. When Ebenezer first arrives at the office of Scrooge & Marley, how many coals does he throw on the fire?

14. Virtually all other versions of *A Christmas Carol* portray the knocker on Scrooge's front door—the one on which he first spies Marley's face—in the shape of a lion's head. However, that is not the case in this adaptation (or was it in Dickens's original story). In the shape of what animal is the doorknocker?

15. When Marley's Ghost asks Scrooge if he's cold, and Ebenezer says yes but refuses to put more coal on the fire because it's "too expensive," what does the Ghost put into the fire instead?

16. Is Scrooge's fiancée called Belle or Adela in this version?

17. What does the sign hanging outside Joe's shop (the establishment where the undertaker and laundress go to sell dead Scrooge's stolen possessions) say?

18. What does the Ghost of Christmas Yet-to-Come look like in this version? Does it speak? Do you see its face?

Jetsons Christmas Carol, A (1985)

19. What business does Mr. Spacely, the Scrooge surrogate for this version, own and operate?

20. What is Mr. Spacely's first name?

21. Where does Elroy Jetson go to school? Judy Jetson?

22. Name Spacely's dead partner.

23. What does the Spirit of Christmas Past look like? The Spirit of Christmas Present?

24. What does the Spirit of Christmas Yet-to-Be look like? Does it talk?

25. What horrible vision does the Spirit of Christmas Yet-to-Be reveal to Mr. Spacely?

26. What Christmas present does Spacely give to Judy Jetson? To Elroy?

27. Name the Jetsons' dog.

28. Who provided the voices of each member of the Jetson family? And who was the voice of Mr. Spacely?

Above, *Scrooge (Michael Caine) and the various Muppet actors.*
Top right, *Rizzo the Rat and the Great Gonzo fly into the past in* The Muppet Christmas Carol *(1993).*
Bottom right, *The holiday spirit amphibian style: Kermit the Frog as Bob Cratchit and a froglet Tiny Tim.*

CHAPTER FOURTEEN

THE MUPPET VERSION

THE MUPPET CHRISTMAS CAROL
(GREAT BRITAIN, 1982) RATING: ★★★

A fast-paced, amusing musical adaptation set in the wacky parallel universe of the world-famous Muppets, *The Muppet Christmas Carol* is probably the best live-action *Carol* available on tape for preschool children. It's funny and imaginative, has acceptable music, and faithfully adheres to Dickens's story (more or less). Plus there are the lovable Muppets to give the entire proceedings a comfortable, familiar ring.

The Muppet Christmas Carol begins with a true feature-length *Carol* first: the entire film is narrated by Charles Dickens himself. Of course, this *is* a Muppet movie, so Charles is portrayed by The Great Gonzo—a blue furry puppet with a long

hooked nose. This nutty narrator then proceeds to relate (and interact with) the story of the only important human being in the plot: Ebenezer Scrooge, played by Michael Caine. Ebenezer, of course, hates Christmas until he's visited by three Ghosts, who persuade him to change his miserly ways toward his kindhearted assistant Bob Cratchit (Kermit the Frog) and Bob's vain, porcine wife (Miss Piggy).

At this point, most adults who haven't already seen this film are probably going to think that the best way to handle *The Muppet Christmas Carol* is to simply plant their kids in front of a TV set, pop in the videocassette and walk away. They shouldn't. Surprisingly, *The Muppet Christmas Carol* has much to interest adults too.

For starters, there's the fact that the Muppets could have taken the easy way out (as did *Mickey's Christmas Carol*) by simply recycling Dickens's story to fit pre-established characters—in this case Kermit the Frog, Miss Piggy, Fozzie Bear, and their Muppet pals. Instead, the filmmakers took chances.

The overall production—which faithfully clings to the original's mid-nineteenth-century locale—has an intriguing blend of slapstick and gravity, whimsy and fear. This hybrid style is reflected in both the storyline and environment; as director Brian Henson put it in the movie's presskit, "This film takes the Muppets, for the first time, into an alternate reality. A fantasy reality, which is not Charles Dickens's London, is not Muppet London, and is not real London. It's something that's a combination of all three; where you believe the Muppets grew up and lived there, just like you believe the people have all grown up and lived there. Our visual concept is all in support of that dynamic mixture."

Visually, the *Muppet Carol is* dynamic. The London on display here is a skewed, crazy place. Humans nonchalantly intermingle with talking horses and singing vegetables; the Ghost of Christmas Past is a small, weird, lambently-lit child who lazily floats in the air amidst a tangle of wispy tattered silk. And movement is everywhere, with lots of bizarre secondary action constantly seeping in and around the corners of the frame. Like that cartful of melons being driven away at film's start, who scream, "Help me! I'm being stolen!"

The Muppet Christmas Carol also is commendable in its refusal to let its storyline degenerate into farce. While it doesn't quite achieve the sublime mixture of comedy and drama attained in *Mr. Magoo's Christmas Carol*, the Muppet version scores high points for the easy manner in which it *does* mix these two contrasting elements.

"At first the idea of doing Dickens with the Muppets was a bit daunting," Brian Henson continues. "But what we found was that the mixture worked stunningly well. The energy of the absurd, irreverent Muppet mentality laid on top of Dickens's sinister and sober world created a wonderful dynamic of its own, one that shot right through the film, from the set design to the wardrobe to the script writing. This new dynamic made it easier than we had thought to stay true to the Muppets while still remaining faithful to Dickens. Which was always our creative compass."

Kermit the Frog and Michael Caine, stars of The Muppet Christmas Carol.

163

Above, *Kermit as Bob Cratchit and two of Scrooge's "rat accountants."* Below, *Miss Piggy as Emily Cratchit (left), along with the rest of her family at Christmas dinner.*

In this respect, Henson and company were completely successful. *The Muppet Christmas Carol* follows the original story quite closely, and, with the inclusion of a poor, shivering rabbit forced to find shelter amidst a litter of snow-covered garbage cans, the film even manages to briefly incorporate Dickens's original social concerns.

Make no mistake, however; there *are* some wild deviations from the original here (like the appearance of *two* ghostly Marleys). But for the most part, these detours are so skillfully done (the beautiful shot of a solitary Kermit singing to a fat, full moon on a deserted London street), or so amusingly inoffensive (Miss Piggy's star-turn as the screeching Emily Cratchit), that even the staunchest *Christmas Carol* purist shouldn't find too much to carp about.

As previously noted, the director of *The Muppet Christmas Carol* was Brian Henson. He is the son of Muppet creator Jim Henson, who was born September 24, 1936 in Greenville, Mississippi, and died May 16, 1990, in New York (incidentally, Jim Henson's earliest TV appearances with the Muppets—we're talking the late-fifties/early sixties—featured his most original and offbeat work).

Brian Henson is also president and chief executive officer of Jim Henson Productions, an organization that has been an established leader in family entertainment for over thirty-five years. Currently, it boasts production facilities in both New York and London. Henson Productions previously produced such popular TV offerings as *The Muppet Show*, a syndicated program which lasted for one hundred twenty episodes, from 1976 to 1981. The company also made films like *The Muppet Movie*, *The Muppets Take Manhattan*, and *The Dark Crystal* (an atypically dark, flawed-but-fascinating work). As for *The Muppet Christmas Carol*, this was the first adaptation ever undertaken by the Henson company; it was also the first time in a movie where the Muppets played characters other than themselves.

The Muppet Christmas Carol's director entered the film business in the late 1970s and began in his father's company. Brian's first jobs were as a puppeteer and "character builder"—Henson-ese for someone who actually *makes* the Muppets. He then began "coordinating performers who did the puppetry. At which point I realized my true artistic passions lay in directing."

The Muppet Christmas Carol subsequently became Brian Henson's first credit as a feature film director. And it's an assured, relaxed debut; besides being a clever retooling of Dickens's classic, this is a marvelously *fluid* film, filled with imaginative, high-tech touches and many curious facts. To wit:

Bob Cratchit and Scrooge encounter two gentlemen (Beaker, left, and Bunsen Honeydew, center) seeking charity for the poor.

- ⚙ The flaming red hair of the Ghost of Christmas Present (a life-size "man in a suit" puppet) slowly turns gray with age as his time with Scrooge grows short.

- ⚙ Nearly one hundred special effects shots were done in the film, like the scene of Scrooge's doorknocker "morphing" (a form of computer animation extensively used in *Terminator 2*) into the face of a dead Marley Brother.

- ⚙ Close to three hundred new Muppet characters were built for the film.

An aging Muppet Ghost of Christmas Present confronts a live Scrooge about his miserly ways.

⊛ Transitions between the past, present, and future are indicated by either dazzling, intricately animated clouds of light or, as in the case of the graveyard scene, the background itself actually *twisting into a spiral* behind Scrooge as he travels between time periods (another startling computer-graphics effect, this one done by Composite Image Systems of Los Angeles).

⊛ All the sets were scaled down to 85 percent of full size in order to accommodate the smaller Muppet proportions.

Which brings us to the music and Michael Caine.

Unfortunately, the curse which hovers over most musical versions of *A Christmas Carol* struck again with the Muppets. The *Muppet Carol*'s songs (by composer Paul Williams) aren't particularly bad, it's just that they're not particularly *good*. Musical "highlights" include Kermit's lead vocals on "One More Sleep 'Til Christmas," and Michael Caine's singing debut on "Thankful Heart" (which won't give Caine a shot at the Metropolitan Opera, but at least proves he can carry a tune).

Overall, the songs herein are only slightly more hummable than the boringly insipid tunes found in the 1970 *Scrooge*. Which leads us to Michael Caine, who plays a not very distinctive Scrooge. To paraphrase my complaint about the music, while there's nothing particularly wrong with Caine's performance, there's nothing to recommend it, either. Playing the miser as a relatively young man, with slightly balding head and long white hair, the best that can be said of Caine's Scrooge is that he proves an adequate foil to the Muppets around him, a sturdy straight man to their anarchic foolishness. Faint praise indeed for the likable, hard-working actor born Maurice Micklewhite (on March 14, 1933, in London), who's delivered exceptional performances in past films like *Zulu* (1964), *The Ipcress File* (1965), *Alfie* (1966), *Get Carter* (1971), *Sleuth* (1972), and *Educating Rita* (1983).

To be fair, however, the emphasis in *The Muppet Christmas Carol* is on the *non-human* performers. So perhaps Michael Caine can be forgiven for his fairly colorless portrayal. Just as one might forgive the occasional adult viewer who, while watching this film, will feel something less than total empathy for a movie filled with hyperactive socks.

Yet despite a curious air of detachment and its ultimate lack of emotional punch, despite its forgettable songs and less-than-captivating Scrooge, *The Muppet Christmas Carol* is *still* a laudable slice of zany entertainment. Kids will love it, adventurous adults will discover something different, and the film itself stands a good chance of becoming a popular Holiday perennial.

Just be sure to check your socks before hanging them up on your fireplace next Christmas, though.

You never know.

One might contain a singing green frog.

Director Brian Henson of The Muppet Christmas Carol.

TRIVIA QUESTIONS
(Answers on page 233)

The Muppet Christmas Carol

1. To whom is *The Muppet Christmas Carol* dedicated? Who are they?

2. What character does Miss Piggy play? Full name, please.

3. The Great Gonzo portrays Charles Dickens in this film. Whom does Rizzo the Rat, Gonzo's sidekick, play?

4. Sticking with Rizzo for a moment, his name is an in-joke reference to another character. One who appeared in a major, late-sixties motion picture. Name this motion picture, the character Rizzo is named after, and the human actor who portrayed that character (HINT: This picture was the only X-rated film to ever win an Oscar).

5. What are Gonzo and Rizzo doing at the start of the film?

6. When he tries to peer into Scrooge and Marley's office, Gonzo discovers that its window is too dirty to see through. What does he use to clean that window?

7. What does Scrooge do to the creditor he finds waiting in his office at the start of the film?

8. What kind of animals play Scrooge's accountants (they're also called bookkeepers)?

9. Unlike any other version of the story, *The Muppet Christmas Carol* presents us with *two* Marleys, who are supposed to be brothers. Name them.

10. At what time does the Ghost of Christmas Past first appear?

11. How do Gonzo and Rizzo follow Scrooge into the past?

12. Four busts of what famous men are seen sitting on a shelf in the boyhood Scrooge's schoolroom?

13. What is under the serving platters tended by the Swedish Chef during Fozziwig's Christmas Party?

14. What party game do the guests play at Scrooge's nephew Fred's Christmas Party?

15. What are the names of Miss Piggy's twin daughters?

16. The Ghost of Christmas Present informs Scrooge that his time on Earth is very short. When does Christmas Present's time end?

17. Why do Gonzo and Rizzo decide to drop out of the Ghost of Christmas Yet-to-Come sequence?

18. What does this Ghost of Christmas Yet-to-Come look like? Do you ever see its face? If so, describe it.

19. What type of animal plays the undertaker?

20. Throughout the film, Scrooge seems totally unaware that Gonzo and Rizzo are following him around and narrating his story. But at one point in the movie, Scrooge *does* acknowledge them. When? And how?

21. What Christmas present does Scrooge give his accountants?

22. What are the last three lines of dialogue in this picture? How do they relate to Dickens's original story?

CHAPTER FIFTEEN

DANCE, SPOKEN-WORD, AND ONE-SHOT VERSIONS

MISCELLANEOUS CAROLS

Here Ye Author rounds up a number of unusual *Carols* that either didn't fit under the categories laid out in the previous chapters, or about which little is known. These are oddities and one-shots, including both spoken-word and dance versions of Dickens's classic!

(For more information on these various entries, particularly the "Spoken-Word" versions, please turn to chapter 17, "Credits and Video Sources.")

Dance Versions

⚛ ***A Christmas Carol*** (1979)

Music, choreography, and live-action combine to give a new interpretation of the story. Videocassette available from Video Outreach.

⚛ ***A Christmas Carol*** (USA, 1982)

A basically dance version of Dickens's classic, performed by the famed Guthrie Theater of Minneapolis company. Occasionally rebroadcast on The Entertainment Channel during the holiday season. Also available on Apollo Video.

⚛ ***A Christmas Carol*** (Australia, 1982)

Yet another dance version of Dickens's novel.

⚛ In 1993, a twenty-minute, modern dance version of Dickens's classic was performed at California State University Long Beach. Titled "Memoirs of a Scrooge," this Master of Fine Arts Thesis project was very well received.

Rock 'n' Roll Carols

⚛ ***Scrooge's Rock 'n' Roll Christmas*** (USA, 1983)

A rock version of Dickens's story, here backed by songs from Rush, Three Dog

Night, and other musical groups. Forty-four minutes long, and available from Sony Video.

Spoken-Word Versions

With the recent surge in popularity of "books on tape," many audiocassette versions of *A Christmas Carol* are now available in bookstores around the country. Some standouts *Carols* in this spoken word format are:

⊛ ***Christmas Carol, A*** (abridged edition). Narrated by Dan O'Herlihy. 2 cassettes. Running Time: 3 hours, 4 mins. Cassette Books.

Noted Irish actor O'Herlihy (who portrayed the head of the ruthless OCP corporation in the first two *RoboCop* films) offers his interpretation of the story.

⊛ ***Christmas Carol, A.*** Narrated by Lionel Barrymore. Performed by Orson Welles. 1 cassette. Running Time: 60 mins. National Recording Company.

Lionel Barrymore! Orson Welles! Together, for the first time, in *A Christmas Carol*! Need Ye Author say more?

⊛ ***Christmas Carol, A.*** Dramatization. Performed by Ralph Richardson and Paul Scofield. 1 cassette. HarperAudio.

Two of England's finest stage actors read Dickens's classic.

- ***Complete Ghost Stories of Charles Dickens.*** Edited by Peter Haining. Read by Jill Masters. 12 cassettes. Running Time: 90 mins. per cassette. Includes "A Christmas Carol," "Captain Murderer and the Devil's Bargain," "The Signal Man," "Queer Chair," "Madman's Manuscript." 1986, Books on Tape. You get not only a good reading of the *Carol* here, but a number of other ghostly Dickens tales as well.

- ***Patrick Stewart Performs Charles Dickens's A Christmas Carol.*** 1991, Simon & Schuster (Cammline Inc). Also available on compact disc.

  Diehard fans of *Star Trek: The Next Generation* know that that show's Captain Picard (Patrick Stewart) has spent the 1990s touring in a well-received one-man version of *A Christmas Carol*, playing all the roles. (He played Broadway for a couple of weeks at the end of 1991 and again in late 1992.) Regrettably, this one-man show is not yet out on video. However, at the time Ye Author wrote this book, Stewart's show could be found on Simon & Schuster audiotapes, as well as on CDs. Look for this product around Christmastime, where other *Star Trek* merchandise is sold.

Miscellaneous Animated and Filmed Christmas Carols

- In 1940, an amateur 8mm short film version of *Carol* was made by Gregory Markopoulos.

- In 1947, a color, six-part animated puppet film called *Czech Year* (original title: *Spalicek*) was made in Czechoslovakia. One of the episodes was *A Christmas Carol* adaptation directed by puppet-master Jiri Trnka.

- In 1960, British director Robert Hartford-Davis directed a short British film titled *A Christmas Carol*. John Hayter played Scrooge.

- 1962 saw the release of a short (twenty-five minutes) British version directed by Desmond Davis. This *Christmas Carol* starred Basil Rathbone as Scrooge and was shot against authentic English backgrounds. (This is *not* the same Rathbone *Carol* as produced as a musical on *The Alcoa Hour* on television in 1956.)

  This 1962 version is available as a video on both the *Coronet* and *MTI Film & Video* labels. Not that Ye Author's been able to find a copy.

- December 21, 1967 witnessed a *Carol*-themed episode on ABC's *Bewitched*, the popular fantasy/sitcom starring Elizabeth Montgomery as Samantha, a witch married to mortal Darren Stevens (portrayed here by Dick York). The title of this episode was "Humbug Not to Be Spoken Here"; it's now available on Columbia TriStar video as *Bewitched Christmas—Volume 1*. In it, Larry Tate (David White), Darren's boss, has Samantha's husband help land an account with "Mortimer Instant Soup." Unfortunately, Mr. Mortimer (Charles Lane) is a modern-day Scrooge for whom "Christmas is just another day." But Samantha

and Santa Claus soon change Mortimer's mind.

⬤ **"A Christmas Story"** (USA, 1979). Animated.

Not the adaptation of Jean Shepard's story about a little boy who dreams of getting a Red Ryder BB gun for Christmas, this was originally broadcast as an episode of comedian Bill Cosby's animated "Fat Albert" cartoon show. And it has strong echoes of Dickens's book.

Story here concerns a mean junkyard owner named Tightwad Tyrone, who plans on demolishing Fat Albert's clubhouse until the Spirit of Christmas gives Tightwad a change of heart. Available from *Barr Films*.

⬤ **"Skinflint"** was a special two-hour *country* version of *A Christmas Carol*, which aired in 1979 on the NBC network.

⬤ Goodtimes Video, which has already released the 1935 and 1951 live-action as well as the 1971 Richard Williams animated version, plans on releasing a fifty-minute, *brand-new animated* Christmas Carol (aimed at children) in September 1994. One *produced* by Goodtimes, certainly the current video-*Carol* champ!

⬤ Which all goes to prove that, if you look hard enough, Scrooge's story can be found just about everywhere!

TRIVIA QUESTIONS
(Answers on page 234)

Miscellaneous Carols

1. In what year did Basil Rathbone find himself playing Scrooge against authentic English backgrounds? Who directed this version?

2. Name the Bill Cosby–created cartoon character who found himself reliving Dickens's story. What was the name of the Scrooge surrogate here?

3. What *Carol* video features performances by the rock groups Three Dog Night and Rush?

4. What dance company has performed its own interpretation of *A Christmas Carol*? Where is this company from?

5. Another curve ball—what is Captain Jean-Luc Picard's favorite beverage?

6. The man who almost played Scrooge in the 1938 version of *A Christmas Carol* joined the director of *Touch of Evil* to perform Dickens's classic on an old radio broadcast, one which is now available as a spoken-word audiocassette. Name these two men.

CHAPTER SIXTEEN

THE WORST VERSION

SCROOGED (USA, 1988) RATING: ★↙

Having now covered so many, many different versions of *A Christmas Carol*—the good, the mundane, and the indifferent—we're left with a (Yule) burning question:

Which is the *worst*?

Could it be the comatose 1969 animated adaptation? The depressing Henry Winkler version? The so-so *Alvin's Christmas Carol*?

The answer to these queries is—none of the above. For only one adaptation *truly* sinks below the rest. This one is a hyperglossy, emotionally dead display of arrogant smugness and persistent ugliness, defects matched only by a relentless sense of tedium.

Our "winner"? *Scrooged*, a 1988 mind-numbing contemporary "comedy" starring Bill Murray.

Seldom has so much been spent to achieve so little.

The recipe behind *Scrooged* must have looked promising on paper. First, take a hot Hollywood star in the person of Bill Murray. Cast him as Frank Cross, ruthless president of the fictitious IBC TV network, a man who hates Christmas and plans to exploit the holidays for every rating point they're worth.

Next hire a successful big-budget director (Richard Donner, *auteur* of the *Lethal Weapon* films). Have him guide Murray through a plot that involves Cross's dead ex-boss (John Forsythe) warning Frank that he'll soon be visited by three Christmas Ghosts—a pointy-eared cabby (David Johansen, who literally drives Cross into his past), a deceptively sweet sugar plum fairy with a mean right hook (Carol Kane), and an enormous skeletal creature who'll scare some holiday spirit back into the IBC exec.

Finally, mix in a handful of supposedly "hip" cameo appearances. Season with dashes of Murray's patented wit, and *voila!*

A sure-fire hit.

Right?

Wrong.

For in the land of misconceived projects, *Scrooged* really is a piece of work.

To begin, this so-called comedy is anything but funny; the laughs are few

Ad art for Scrooged.

and far between. Even more bewilderingly, *especially* for an adaptation of as sentimental and life-affirming a story as *A Christmas Carol*, the primary emotions of *Scrooged* are rage and disgust.

Ye Author supposes that on a subtextual level, *Scrooged* could be read as a thinly disguised hate letter aimed at everything mercenary about Yuppie greediness. Or at everything that's hateful about the repulsive Machiavellian manipulations lurking behind Hollywood's façade. Unfortunately, much of this hatred is aimed at the *viewer*, not at the film's so-called satirical targets.

Take the case of Cross's character. *Scrooged* begins with Murray caught up in a career crisis. His equally venal network president, Preston Rhinelander (Robert Mitchum), has just brought in a smarmy West Coast producer (John Glover) to "help" Cross oversee the live broadcast of an all-star "Christmas Carol" show, one that Cross planned to produce himself. But Cross suspects that Rhinelander's action is really a thinly disguised signal that the big boss has lost faith in him. And as Cross's stress over his job insecurity escalates, so does his outrageously despicable behavior (and it *is* despicable; Murray deserves some sort of no-prize for portraying the screen's most hateful Scrooge).

Now, we all understand the fear of job loss. So we're also supposed to forgive Cross's nastiness, since it's based on insecurity. Which would be a sound rationale if Cross were a believable human being. Or if he had any redeeming qualities. Even *one*.

The Ghost of Christmas Present (Carol Kane) preparing to give the obnoxious Frank Cross (Bill Murray) a lesson in the holiday spirit—by poking him in the eyeballs!

But throughout most of *Scrooged*, Cross is portrayed as an appallingly critical, miserably cruel, abnormally self-centered weasel. Worse, Murray's performance lacks his usual self-deprecating good humor, the sly little signals that let you know he's just kidding around with the character.

This lack of humor—of *heart*—throws the whole film out of whack. Nowhere is this more apparent than in *Scrooged*'s loopy conclusion. Here a supposedly reformed Cross walks onto a TV soundstage to deliver a speech about the true spirit of Christmas. What pours out of his mouth doesn't sound like the heartfelt confessions of a humbled, spiritually transformed convert, though. Instead, we're subjected to the rambling, disjointed ravings of a short-circuited lunatic.

The *words* are there, but Cross's speech (which goes on far too long) is completely lacking in any conviction, warmth, or sincerity. And when Cross demands a miracle—and is instantly rewarded with one, on cue, by a heretofore mute little black boy, who suddenly pipes up with an irrelevant "God Bless us, everyone!"—one has to wonder what the screenwriters were smoking that day.

There's more (a *lot* more) to criticize here, like the forced, unbelievable, and unending singalong of "Put a Little Love in Your Heart," into which the entire cast breaks at film's end. But why bother? This *is* a book about *A Christmas Carol* after all. The overriding message of which is "goodwill toward men."

So for Bill Murray's friends and relatives—as well as for the half-dozen or so other people who might actually *like* this cold, repulsive thing—here are a few inter-

Bill Murray and David Johansen as the cab-driving Ghost of Christmas Past.

esting (maybe even *nice*) comments Ye Author can make about *Scrooged*:

- ✸ The film opens with a clever jab at showbiz crassness, as a roomful of solemn TV executives watch a proposed program about Santa's Workshop falling siege to a band of heavily armed terrorists. The program's title? "The Night the Reindeer Died."

- ✸ Cross's "Christmas Carol" broadcast stars Buddy Hackett as Ebenezer Scrooge and former Olympic gymnast Mary Lou Retton as Tiny Tim—a fairly droll piece of offbeat casting, even if these performers don't seem to know that the (rather nasty) joke's on them.

- ✸ Michael Chapman's sleek cinematography gives *Scrooged* an appropriately dark, velvety look.

- ✸ The film has a *très bizarre* string of cameo appearances, everyone from jazz legend Miles Davis to lounge singer Robert Goulet.

- ✸ *Scrooged*'s cast includes all three of Bill Murray's brothers. Brian Doyle Murray portrays Frank Cross's father (in a scene from Christmas Past), John Murray plays Cross's younger brother James (in the present), and Joel Murray is a guest at the Christmas party hosted by James and his wife.

- ✸ The decaying corpse of John Forsythe dangling Cross above the sidewalks of

New York—after first pushing him through a high-rise windowpane that magical-ly parts around Murray like water—is an impressive supernatural touch.

⊛ The Checker Cab transporting Cross into the past has a meter that doesn't ring up a fare; it counts back the *years* instead.

⊛ The moment when Cross discovers the frozen corpse of a smiling derelict in a subterranean sewer actually provokes a genuine shudder (one of the film's few effective scenes).

⊛ The Ghost of Christmas Future first appears on a huge "video wall" (a wide bank of television monitors), and his entrance is an inspired visual touch.

⊛ Production designer J. Michael Riva (grandson of Marlene Dietrich; Maria Riva, Michael's mother, is in the movie as Mitchum's wife) also worked with director Richard Donner on *Lethal Weapon*, and was Oscar-nominated for *The Color Purple*.

⊛ Tom Burman and Bari Dreiband-Burman, who also provided makeup services for *Close Encounters of the Third Kind* and the 1978 remake of *Invasion of the Body Snatchers*, did the special makeup effects for *Scrooged*. Which included building an intricately articulated Ghost of Christmas Yet-to-Come, one whose open robe reveals wailing faces growing out of its chest (altogether, three

Bill Murray and director Richard Donner consult on more ways to trash A Christmas Carol.

183

differently-sized Future Ghosts were constructed by the Burmans; each was operated by a combination of puppetry, hydraulics, and electronics).

⚙ Composer Danny Elfman, who previously did the scores for *Beetlejuice*, *Batman*, and *The Simpsons*, provided a lively musical soundtrack for *Scrooged*.

⚙ Director Richard Donner cameos as an IBC cameraman.

Yet the absolute *best* thing about this film is Carol Kane. A two-time Emmy Award winner, born June 18, 1952, in Cleveland, she's best known for her role as the daffy Eastern European immigrant Simka Gravas on the long-running *Taxi* TV show. And it's her sweetly crazy performance as the Ghost of Christmas Present—a winged, wand-waving fairy who alternately kicks, slaps, and punches Cross all around Manhattan—that gives *Scrooged* what little sparkle it has.

"I thought of Christmas Present as sort of a wild version of Glinda the Good Witch, from *The Wizard of Oz*," Kane explained in the *Scrooged* production notes. "She's a good fairy who resorts to any and all methods of accomplishing her mission. And it really was a dream come true to play a part like this. When I was a little girl I dreamt of getting to wear glitter and wings and of flying around with a wand. But Bill (Murray) certainly did take a fair amount of abuse from me, because I'd never done any stunt work before. I slapped him. I pulled his hair, cheeks, and lips. And I tweaked his nose. Bill was very patient, though. Because I knew it hurt."

Cross's dead boss Lew Hayward (John Forsythe) dangles him high above the city streets.

Kane's hilarious turn as the Christmas Present Ghost is, unfortunately, the only small oasis of life in that otherwise vast celluloid desert called *Scrooged*. This mean-spirited exercise in wretched excess is not only the worst *Christmas Carol* committed to film, it's also a painful audience endurance test.

Even for the most dedicated bad-movie masochist.

As Ebenezer Scrooge himself would have surely said:

"Bah, humbug!"

TRIVIA QUESTIONS
(Answers on page 234)

Scrooged

1. What's the name of the proposed Christmas special being watched by the IBC Network brass at the start of this film? The one where Santa's workshop is threatened by terrorists?

2. Who plays Scrooge in the *Christmas Carol* TV special Bill Murray is producing? Who plays Tiny Tim?

3. What Christmas presents does Murray give his secretary Grace?

4. Who plays the Jacob Marley surrogate here? What is this character's name?

John Forsythe as the Jacob Marley surrogate. Makeup by Tom and Bari Burman.

5. At what time does the Ghost of Christmas Present appear? What's his occupation? What's on his license plate?

6. Name the real-life Tiny Tim surrogate here (not the Mary Lou Retton character: the *other* Tiny Tim). What's his physical affliction, and how did he come by it?

7. Give the Bill Murray character's full name. Plus his occupation and nickname.

8. When a stagehand complains to Cross that he can't hot-glue a pair of antlers on a mouse's head, what does Cross suggest he do instead?

9. During the 1969 Christmas Past segment, what present do we see Cross giving his girlfriend Claire?

10. How does the Ghost of Christmas Present transport Cross from one location to another?

11. What is Calvin, the mute black boy, watching on his family's TV set during the Christmas Present sequence?

12. What does this Ghost of Christmas Yet-to-Come look like? Do you ever see its face? Does it talk?

13. Name the song that runs over the *Scrooged* end credits.

CHAPTER SEVENTEEN
CREDITS AND
VIDEO SOURCES

The following chapter fulfills two functions: scholarship and commerce. Listed herein are all available credits (cast, director, running times, etc.) of the various film, dance, animated, rock 'n' roll and TV versions of *A Christmas Carol* mentioned in this book.

Ye Author has also included a separate section on audiocassette *Carols* cataloguing spoken-word readings of the story. Those versions which Ye Author feels have particular merit are indicated by an asterisk (*) before the title; information in these entries also include who reads or performs the story, the overall running time of the audiotape, and which company released it.

This chapter also indicates whether a film or television (or whatever) version of *A Christmas Carol* is available on *video*tape. The names of the companies

which have released *Carols* on video are also listed at the end of each title.

Sadly, throughout this chapter you will come across the symbol N/A. This means "Not Available." It pertains to the fact that either a specific title is not available on videotape, or that some specific information on that title (such as the name of a director or cast member) is unknown at the time of the writing of this book.

Ye Author now guiltily admits that there is still a great deal of information to be uncovered on the various versions of *A Christmas Carol*. His only defense is that this book was an exploration into relatively uncharted waters; until now, no volume *solely concerned* with this many versions of *A Christmas Carol* has ever seen print. Nevertheless, territory has been charted by others as part of larger expeditions; witness William Leonard's *Theatre: Stage to Screen to Television* (Scarecrow, 1982) and Alvin H. Marill's *More Theatre: Stage to Screen to Television* (Scarecrow, 1993), two exhaustive multi-volume chronicles of every significant theatrical production in the English language (excluding Shakespeare and a few other old-timers) and each play's subsequent adaptation to film and television.

However, Ye Author also hopes that his *Trivia* book, like *A Christmas Carol* itself, will continue to grow in recognition and popularity. Therefore, any reader who might know of *any "Christmas Carol" not covered in this book*, or who may know *specific credit information not included in this section* (say, the running time of the 1901 silent version), is urged to contact Ye Author immediately. He will then incorporate any worthwhile information concerned readers mail in for the

next edition of this book. Plus, readers who do contribute new information will be so acknowledged in the next, updated printing of *The Christmas Carol Trivia Book*.

Please indicate, when writing, exactly what type of *Carol* you are bringing to Ye Author's attention (a film version, television version, etc.). Send all information, queries, and letters to:

The Christmas Carol Trivia Book
Attn: Paul M. Sammon
c/o Carol Publishing Group
600 Madison Avenue
New York, NY 10022

Don't forget—this is *your* chance to help spread Christmas cheer throughout America. *And* the chance to see your name in print!

Finally, since so much credit and video information is covered in this chapter, a short listing of where you can find that information, (and under what category) would seem to be in order.

So here it is. A mini–table of contents, if you will.

The various *Christmas Carol* adaptations presented in chapter 17 are, in order: 1. Films 2. Television 3. Animated 4. Dance 5. Rock 'n' Roll 6. Spoken-Word

Films

Christmas Carol, A (aka *Scrooge*) (Great Britain, 1901) N/A SILENT B&W ? mins.
Director: W. R. Booth. Starring: N/A
Videocassette Source: N/A

Christmas Carol, A (USA,1908) N/A SILENT B&W ? mins.
Director: N/A Starring: Thomas Ricketts.
Videocassette Source: N/A

Christmas Carol, A (USA, 1910) N/A SILENT B&W 17 mins.
Director: Ashley Miller [some sources credit J. Searle Dawley]. (Produced by Thomas Edison). Starring: Charles Ogle, William Bechtel, Carey Lee.
Videocassette Source: N/A

Christmas Carol, A (USA, 1912) N/A SILENT B&W ? mins.
Director: N/A Starring: N/A
Videocassette Source: N/A

Christmas Carol, A (aka *Scrooge*) Great Britain, 1913) N/A SILENT B&W 50 mins.

Director: Leedham Bantock. Screenplay: Seymour Hicks. Starring: Seymour Hicks, William Lugg, J. C. Buckstone, Dorothy Buckstone, Leedham Bantock, Leonard Calvert, Osborne Adair, Adela Measor.
Videocassette Source: N/A

Christmas Carol, A (Great Britain, 1914) N/A SILENT B&W 22 mins.
Director: Harold Shaw. Screenplay: Harold Shaw. Starring: Charles Rock, George Bellamy, Mary Brough, Franklyn Bellamy, Edward O'Neill, Edna Flugrath, Arthur Cullin.
Videocassette Source: N/A

Christmas Carol, A (Great Britain, 1935) SEE *Scrooge (1935)*

Christmas Carol, A (USA, 1938) * * * B&W 69 mins.
Director: Edwin L. Marin. Screenplay: Hugo Butler. Starring: Reginald Owen, Gene Lockhart, Terry Kilburn, Leo G. Carroll, Lionel Braham, Lynne Carver, Anne Rutherford, Barry Mackay, Kathleen Lockhart, June Lockhart.
Videocassette Source: MGM/UA HOME VIDEO

Christmas Carol (USA, 1940)   N/A   AMATEUR SHORT   (16mm)   N/A   ? mins.
Director: Gregory Markopoulos. Starring: N/A
Videocassette Source: N/A

Christmas Carol, A (Spain, 1947)   N/A   B&W   ? mins.
Director: Manuel Tamayo. Starring: Tordesillas, Lina Yergos, Requena, Joaquin Soler Serrano, Angel Picazo.
Videocassette Source: N/A

Christmas Carol, A (aka *Scrooge*) (Great Britain, 1951)   * * * *   B&W   83 mins.
Director: Brian Desmond-Hurst.
Screenplay: Noel Langley. Starring: Alastair Sim, Mervyn Johns, Jack Warner, Kathleen Harrison, Michael Hordern, Miles Malleson, Francis De Wolff, Patrick Macnee.
Videocassette Source: GOODTIMES HOME VIDEO PLATINUM SERIES (SP SPEED), GOODTIMES HOME VIDEO (LP SPEED), VCI HOME VIDEO, UNITED HOME VIDEO

Christmas Carol, A (Great Britain, 1960)   N/A   SHORT   B&W   28 mins.

Director: Robert Hartford-Davis. Starring: John Hayter, Stewart Brown, Gordon Mulholland.
Videocassette Source: N/A

Christmas Carol, A (Great Britain, 1962)   N/A   SHORT   B&W   25 mins.
Director: Desmond Davis. Starring: Basil Rathbone.
Videocassette Source: CORONET VIDEO/MTI FILM & VIDEO

Czech Year (aka *Spalicek*) (Czechoslovakia, 1947)   N/A   COLOR   ? mins.
Director: Jiri Trnka. Starring: N/A
Videocassette Source: N/A

Dream of Old Scrooge, The (Italy, 1910)   N/A   SILENT   B&W   10 mins.
Director: N/A   Starring: N/A
Videocassette Source: N/A

Muppet Christmas Carol, The (Great Britain, 1992)   * * *   COLOR   85 mins.
Director: Brian Henson. Screenplay: Jerry Juhl. Starring: Michael Caine, The Great Gonzo, Rizzo the Rat, Kermit the Frog,

Miss Piggy, Fozzie Bear, Assorted Muppets (Vocal performances by Frank Oz, Dave Goelz, Jerry Nelson, Richard Hunt). Videocassette Source: WALT DISNEY HOME VIDEO

Old Scrooge (Italy, 1910)   N/A   SILENT   B&W   12 mins.
Director: N/A   Starring: N/A
Videocassette Source: N/A

Right to Be Happy, The (USA, 1916)   N/A   SILENT   B&W   60 mins.
Director: Rupert Julian. Screenplay: Rupert Julian. Starring: Rupert Julian, John Cook, Claire McDowell, Frankie Lee, Harry Carter, Emory Johnson.
Videocassette Source: N/A

Scrooge (aka *A Christmas Carol*) SEE *Christmas Carol, A* (1901)

Scrooge (aka *A Christmas Carol*) SEE *Christmas Carol, A* (1913)

Scrooge (Great Britain, 1923) N/A SILENT B&W 2 reels.
Director: W. C. Rowden. Screenplay: W. C.

Rowden. Starring: Russell Thorndike, Jack Denton, Nina Vanna, Forbes Dawson.
Videocassette Source: N/A

Scrooge (aka *Christmas Carol, A*) (Great Britain, 1935)   * * *   B&W   78(60) mins.
Director: Henry Edwards. Screenplay: Seymour Hicks, H. Fowler Mear. Starring: Seymour Hicks, Donald Calthrop, Barbara Everest, Philip Frost, Mary Glynne, Robert Cocha, Marie Nye, Oscar Ashe, Maurice Evans.
Videocassette Source: GOODTIMES VIDEO, VIKING VIDEO CLASSICS, MOVIE BUFF VIDEO: VIDEO YESTERYEAR: BLACKHAWK FILMS: DISCOUNT VIDEO TAPE

Scrooge (aka *A Christmas Carol*) SEE *Christmas Carol, A* (1951)

Scrooge (Great Britain, 1970)   * * 1/2   COLOR   118 mins.
Director: Ronald Neame. Screenplay: Leslie Bricusse. Starring: Albert Finney, Alec Guinness, Edith Evans, Kenneth More, Laurence Naismith, Michael Medwin,

David Collings, Gordon Jackson, Roy Kinnear, Kay Walsh.
Videocassette Source: CBS/FOX VIDEO

Scrooged (USA, 1988) *1/2 COLOR
101 mins.
Director: Richard Donner. Screenplay: Mitch Glazer, Michael O'Donoghue. Starring: Bill Murray, Karen Allen, John Forsythe, John Glover, Bobcat Goldthwait, David Johansen, Carol Kane, Robert Mitchum, Alfre Woodard, Buddy Hackett, John Houseman, Brian Doyle-Murray, Mary Lou Retton, Michael J. Pollard.
Videocassette Source: PARAMOUNT HOME VIDEO

Television

American Christmas Carol, An (Canada, 1979) * *1/2 ABC COLOR
97 mins.
Director: Eric Till. Starring: Henry Winkler, David Wayne, Chris Wiggins, R. H. Thomson, Kenneth Pogue, Gerard Parkes, Susan Hogan, Dorian Harewood

(Special Makeup by Rick Baker).
Videocassette Source: VESTRON VIDEO

Bewitched–"Humbug Not to Be Spoken Here" (on tape as *Bewitched Christmas–Volume 1*) (USA, 1967) * * 1/2 ABC COLOR
25 mins.
Director: N/A Starring: Elizabeth Montgomery, Dick York, Charles Lane, Don Beddoe.
Videocassette Source: COLUMBIA TRISTAR HOME VIDEO

Blackadder's Christmas Carol (Great Britain, 1988) * * * BBC
COLOR 43 mins.
Director: Richard Boden. Starring: Rowan Atkinson, Tony Robinson, Robbie Coltrane, Miranda Richardson, Hugh Laurie, Stephen Fry, Miriam Margolyes, Jim Broadbent, Nicola Bryant.
Videocassette Source: FOX VIDEO

Carol for Another Christmas (USA, 1964) N/A ABC B&W 90 mins.
Director: Joseph L. Mankiewicz. Teleplay:

Rod Serling. Starring: Sterling Hayden, Ben Gazzara, Peter Sellers, Eva Marie Saint, Steve Lawrence, Pat Hingle, Robert Shaw, Britt Ekland, James Shigeta, Percy Rodriques.
Videocassette Source: N/A

Christmas at the Movies (USA, 1990)
N/A   SYNDICATED DOCUMENTARY
B&W/COLOR   60 mins.
Director: Jennifer Libbee. Host: Gene Kelly. Appearances By: Seymour Hicks, Rich Little, Mr. Magoo, Henry Winkler.
Videocassette Source: COLUMBIA TRI-STAR HOME VIDEO

"Christmas Carol" (USA, 1945)   N/A
CHICAGO , STATION WBKB B&W   ? mins.
Director: N/A   Starring: N/A
Videocassette Source: N/A

"Christmas Carol, A" (USA, 1947)   N/A
DUMONT NETWORK   B&W   60 mins.
Director: James L. Caddigan. Starring: John Carradine, Barnard Hughes, Eva Marie Saint.
Videocassette Source: N/A

"Christmas Carol, A" (on *Philco Television Playhouse*) (USA,19481948)
N/A   NBC   B&W   60 mins.
Director: Gordon Duff. Starring: Dennis King, Frank M. Thomas, Valerie Cossart, John Baragray, Dennis King Jr., Loring Smith, James MacColl.
Videocassette Source: N/A

"Christmas Carol, A" (on *Fireside Theatre*) (USA, 1951)   N/A   NBC   B&W   30 mins.
Director: Gordon Duff. Starring: Ralph Richardson, Margaret Phillips, Arthur Treacher, Melville Cooper, Malcolm Keene, Robert Hay Smith, Norman Barr.
Videocassette Source: N/A

"Christmas Carol, A" (on *Kraft Television Theater*) (USA, 1952)   N/A
NBC   B&W   60 mins.
Director: Fielder Cook. Starring: Malcolm Keene, Harry Townes, Valerie Cossart, Glenn Walker, Richard Purdy, Melville Cooper, Noel Leslie.
Videocassette Source: N/A

"Christmas Carol, A" (on *Kraft Television Theater*) (USA, 1953) N/A NBC B&W 60 mins.
Director: Fielder Cook. Starring: Melville Cooper, Noel Leslie, Denis Greene, Harry Townes, Geoffrey Lumb, Valerie Cossart.
Videocassette Source: N/A

"Christmas Carol, A" (on *Eye On New York*) (USA, 1955) N/A NEW YORK N/A B&W ? mins.
Director: N/A Starring: N/A
Videocassette Source: N/A

Christmas Carol, A (Great Britain, 1962) N/A BBC B&W ? mins.
Director: N/A Starring: N/A
Videocassette Source: N/A

Christmas Carol, A (Great Britain, 1984) * * * 1/2 CBS COLOR 100 mins.
Director: Clive Donner. Teleplay: Roger O. Hirson. Starring: George C. Scott, Frank Finlay, Nigel Davenport, David Warner, Susannah York, Anthony Walters, Edward Woodward, Angela Pleasence, Lucy Gutteridge, Roger Rees.
Videocassette Source: N/A

"Christmas Carol, Part Two, A" (on *George Burns Comedy Week*) (USA,1985) N/A CBS COLOR 30 mins.
Director: N/A Starring: James Whitmore, Ed Begley Jr., Roddy McDowall.
Videocassette Source: N/A

Christmas Present (Great Britain, 1985) N/A BBC COLOR ? mins.
Director: Tony Bicat. Starring: Peter Chelsom, Bill Fraser.
Videocassette Source: N/A

Dickens Christmas Carol. (USA, 1948) N/A NEW YORK, ABC B&W ? mins.
Director: N/A Starring: N/A
Videocassette Source: N/A

John Grin's Christmas (USA, 1986) N/A ABC COLOR 60 mins.
Director: Robert Guillaume. Starring: Robert Guillaume, Roscoe Lee Browne, Ted Lange, Alfonso Ribiero, Geoffrey Holder, Candy Ann Brown.

Videocassette Source: N/A

"Mr. Scrooge" (USA, 1964)   N/A   N/A
   B&W   ? mins.
   Director: N/A   Starring: N/A
   Videocassette Source: N/A

Rich Little's Christmas Carol (Canada,
   1978)   * *   CBC (CANADIAN BROAD
   CASTING CORPORATION)   COLOR
   50 mins.
   Director: Trevor Edwards. Starring: Rich
   Little.
   Videocassette Source: SVS INC.

"Skinflint" (USA, 1979)   N/A
   NBC   COLOR   120 mins.
   Director: Marc Daniels. Starring: Hoyt
   Axton, Mel Tillis, Lynn Anderson, Dottie
   West, Barbara Mandrell, Larry Gatlin,
   Martha Raye, Danny Davis and the
   Nashville Brass.
   Videocassette Source: N/A

"Spirit of Christmas, The" (on *Shower of
   Stars*) (USA, 1954)   * * *   CBS
   COLOR   (VIDEO IN B&W)   60 mins.

Director: Ralph Levy. Teleplay: Maxwell
Anderson. Starring: Fredric March, Basil
Rathbone, Bob Sweeney, Ray Middleton,
Queenie Leonard, Christopher Cook,
William Lundigan (Host).
Videocassette Source: VIKING VIDEO CLAS-
   SICS, CAROUSEL FILM & VIDEO

"Stingiest Man in Town, The" (on *The
   Alcoa Hour*) (USA, 1956)   N/A
   NBC   B&W   90 mins.
   Director: Daniel Petrie. Starring: Basil
   Rathbone, Vic Damone, Patrice Munsel,
   Martyn Green, Dennis Kohler, Johnny
   Desmond, The Four Lads.
   Videocassette Source: N/A

"Trail to Christmas, The" (on *The General
   Electric Theater*) (USA, 1957)
   N/A   CBS   B&W   26 mins.
   Director: James Stewart. Starring: Richard
   Eyer, John McIntire, James Stewart, Sam
   Edwards, Will Wright, Kevin Hagen,
   Dennis Holmes.
   Videocassette Source: N/A

Animated

Alvin's Christmas Carol (USA, 1989) * *
   COLOR   23 mins.
   Director: N/A   Starring the Voices of:
   Ross Bagdasarian, Janice Karman, Thom
   Watkins, Dody Goodman.
   Videocassette Source: BUENA VISTA HOME
   VIDEO

Br'er Rabbit's Christmas Carol (USA, ?)
   N/A   COLOR   ? mins.
   Director: N/A   Starring the Voices of: N/A
   Videocassette Source: VIDEO TREASURES,
   SABAN VIDEO

Christmas Carol, A (USA,   1966)
   N/A   N/A   ? mins.
   Director: N/A   Starring: N/A
   Videocassette Source: N/A

Christmas Carol, A (Australia, 1969) * 1/2
   CBS   COLOR   46 mins.
   Director: Zoran Janjic. Starring the Voices
   of: Ron Haddrick, Bruce Montague, John
   Llewellyn, Brenda Senders, C. Duncan, T.
   Mangan. Singing By: T. Kaff, C. Bowden.
   Videocassette Source: RHINO HOME VIDEO

Christmas Carol, A (USA/Great Britain,
   1971)   RATING: * * *   ABC
   COLOR   26 mins.
   Director & Producer: Richard Williams.
   Executive Producer: Chuck Jones. Starring
   the Voices of: Alastair Sim, Sir Michael
   Redgrave, Michael Hordern, Diana Quick,
   Joan Sims, Paul Whitsun-Jones, David
   Tate, Felix Felton, Annie West, Melvyn
   Hayes, Mary Ellen Ray.
   Videocassette Source: GOODTIMES
   VIDEO/"KIDS KLASSICS" HOME VIDEO

Christmas Carol, A (Australia, 1982) * *
   COLOR   72 mins.
   Director: Jean Tych. Starring the Voices of:
   Ron Haddrick, Robin Stewart, Barbara
   Frawley, Sean Hinton, Phillip Hinton, Liz
   Horne, Bill Conn, Derani Scarr, Anne
   Haddy.
   Videocassette Source: VESTRON VIDEO (THE
   CHARLES DICKENS COLLECTION), CHILDREN'S
   VIDEO LIBRARY

Christmas Carol, A (1994)   N/A
   COLOR   50 mins.
   Director: N/A   Starring the Voices of: N/A

Videocassette Source: GOODTIMES VIDEO

Christmas Story, A (USA, 1979)   N/A
COLOR   23 mins.
Director: N/A   Starring the Voices of: Bill
Cosby, N/A.
Videocassette Source: BARR FILMS

"Jetsons Christmas Carol, A" (USA, 1985)
* * 1/2   COLOR   23 mins.
Director: N/A   Starring the Voices of:
George O'Hanlon, Penny Singleton, Janet
Waldo, Daws Butler, Don Messick, Jean
Vanderpyl, Frank Welker, Mel Blanc.
Videocassette Source: HANNA-BARBERA HOME
VIDEO

Making of Mickey's Christmas Carol, The
(USA, 1984)   * * 1/2   COLOR
24 mins.
Director: NOT CREDITED. Starring: Alan
Young, Clarence Nash, Bernie Mattinson,
Mark Henn, Wayne Allwine, Jimmy
MacDonald, Hal Smith.
Videocassette Source: WALT DISNEY HOME
VIDEO

Mickey's Christmas Carol (USA, 1983)
* * 1/2   COLOR   26 mins.
Director: Bernie Mattinson. Starring the
Voices of: Alan Young, Clarence Nash,
Wayne Allwine, Hal Smith.
Videocassette Source: WALT DISNEY HOME
VIDEO, WALT DISNEY'S MINI-CLASSICS

Mr. Magoo's Christmas Carol (USA, 1962)
* * * 1/2   COLOR   52 mins.
Director: Abe Levitow. Starring the Voices
of: Jim Backus, Morey Amsterdam, Jack
Cassidy, Royal Dano, Paul Frees, Jane
Keen, Les Tremayne.
Videocassette Source: PARAMOUNT HOME
VIDEO

Stingiest Man in Town, The (USA, 1978)
N/A   COLOR   60 mins.
Director: Jules Bass, Arthur Rankin
Jr. Starring the Voices of: Walter Matthau,
Tom Bosley, Robert Morse, Dennis Day,
Theodore Bikel, Debra Clinger, Charlie
Matthau, Shelby Flint, Paul Frees.
Videocassette Source: N/A

Dance

Christmas Carol, A (?, 1979)   N/A
    DANCE   COLOR   90 mins.
Director: N/A   Starring: N/A
Videocassette Source: VIDEO OUTREACH

Christmas Carol, A (USA, 1982)   N/A
    DANCE   COLOR   90 mins.
Director: Paul Miller. Starring: Richard
Hilger, J. Patrick Martin, Jonathan Fuller,
Peter Thoemke, Stephen D'Ambrose.
Videocassette Source: APOLLO VIDEO

Christmas Carol, A (Australia, 1982)
    N/A DANCE N/A ? mins.
Director: N/A   Starring: N/A
Videocassette Source: N/A

Rock 'n' Roll

Scrooge's Rock 'n' Roll Christmas (USA,
    1983) N/A ROCK 'N' ROLL
    COLOR   44 mins.
Director: N/A   Starring: Three Dog Night
(rock group), Rush (rock group).
Videocassette Source: SONY VIDEO SOFTWARE

Spoken-Word

*Christmas Carol, A (unabridged edition)
    Read by Richard Green. 3 cassettes.
    Running Time: 3 hours. 1984, Books
    on Tape.

Christmas Carol, A
    Performed by Rick Cimino & Bernard
    Mayes. 1 cassette. Running time: 1
    hour. 1972, Mind's Eye CA.

Christmas Carol, A (unabridged edition)
    Read by Gene Engene. 2 cassettes.
    Running time: 3 hours. Books in
    Motion.

Christmas Carol, A (unabridged edition)
    Read by Frank Muller. 2 cassettes.
    Running time: 3 hours. 1980,
    Recorded Books.

Christmas Carol, A (unabridged edition)
    Read by Flo Gibson. 2 cassettes.
    Running time: 90 mins. per cassette.
    Audio Book Connection.

Christmas Carol, A (abridged edition)
    Performed by Tom Conti. 1 cassette.

Running time: N/A. HarperAudio.

Christmas Carol, A (abridged edition)
Narrated by Dan O'Herlihy. 2 cas-
settes. Running time: 3 hours, 4 mins.
Cassette Books.

Christmas Carol, A
Narrated by Lionel Barrymore.
Performed by OrsonWelles. 1 cassette.
Running time: 60 mins. National
Recording Company.

Christmas Carol, A (unabridged edition)
Dramatization. 1 cassette. Running
time: 56 mins. 1978, Jimcin
Recordings.

Christmas Carol, A (unabridged edition)
Read by Robert L. Halvorson. 2 cas-
settes. Running time: 3 hours.
Halvorson Associates.

Christmas Carol, A (abridged edition)
Read by Frank Pettingell. 1 cassette.
Running time: 47 mins. Spoken Arts.

Christmas Carol, A (abridged edition)
Read by Leonard Rossiter. 2 read-along

cas-   settes. Running time: 2 hours. 1986,
Durkin Hayes Pub.

Christmas Carol, A
Read by John Gielgud. 1987, Bantam.

Christmas Carol, A
1 cassette. Running time: 1 hour. 1987,
Radiola Co.

Christmas Carol, A 1 cassette. 1988, Troll
Associates.

Christmas Carol, A (abridged edition)
Read by Paul Scofield. 2 cassettes.
Running time: 3 hours. 1989, Dove
Audio.

Christmas Carol, A
3 cassettes. Ulvscrft Sounds.

Christmas Carol, A
Durkin Hayes.

Christmas Carol, A
Read by Michael Low. 3 cassettes.
Running time: 90 mins. per cassette
Blackstone Audio.

Christmas Carol, A
Dramatization. Performed by Ralph

Richardson and Paul Scofield. 1 cassette. Harper Audio.

Complete Ghost Stories of Charles Dickens Edited by Peter Haining. Read by Jill Masters. 12 cassettes. Running time: 90 mins. per cassette. Includes "A Christmas Carol," "Captain Murderer and the Devil's Bargain," "The Signal Man," "Queer Chair," "Madman's Manuscript." 1986, Books on Tape.

Patrick Stewart Performs Charles Dickens's "A Christmas Carol." 1991, Cammline Inc. Also available on compact disc.

CHAPTER EIGHTEEN

BIBLIOGRAPHY

By now, you're probably thinking Ye Author has *got* to be an obsessive *Christmas Carol* nut.

Well, you're right.

But even obsessives couldn't carry *this* much information in their heads.

The following bibliography recounts the most important reference works utilized during the compilation of *The "Christmas Carol" Trivia Book*. Those interested in further information on Charles Dickens, *A Christmas Carol*, or its various incarnations should consult the various (recommended) books and periodicals listed here.

Happy browsing!

Books

American Animated Cartoon, The, by Gerald and Danny Peary. E.P. Dutton, 1980.

Animated Film, The, by Ralph Stephenson. The Tantivy Press/A.S. Barnes & Co., 1981.

Annotated Christmas Carol, The, by Michael Patrick Hearn. Clarkson N. Potter, Inc. 1976.

"B" Directors, The: A Biographical Directory, by Wheeler W. Dixon. The Scarecrow Press, 1985.

Christmas Tales, by Charles Dickens. Dodd, Mead & Company, 1941.

Cinema Sequels and Remakes 1903–1987, by Robert A. Nowlan & Gwendolyn Wright Nowlan. McFarland & Company, 1989.

Complete Directory of Prime Time TV Stars, The, by Tim Brooks. Ballantine Books, 1987.

Dickens, by Peter Ackroyd. HarperCollins, 1990.

Encyclopedia of Animated Cartoons, The, by Jeff Lenburg. Facts on File, 1991.

Encyclopedia of Television Specials, Pilots and Specials, 1937–1973, by Vincent Terrace. New York Zoetrope, 1986.

Film Directors: A Complete Guide, Eighth Annual International Edition, compiled and edited by Michael Singer. Lone Eagle Press, 1989.

Film Encyclopedia, The, by Ephraim Katz. Perigee Books/G. P. Putnam's Sons, 1979.

Five Christmas Novels, by Charles Dickens. The Heritage Press, 1939.

Harry and Wally's Favorite TV Shows, by Harry Castleman and Walter J. Podrazik. Prentice-Hall Press, 1989.

Horror and Science Fiction Films: A Checklist, by Donald C. Willis. The Scarecrow Press, 1972.

Illustrated Who's Who of the Cinema, The, edited by Anne Lloyd, Graham Fuller and Arnold Desser. Macmillan, 1983.

Leonard Maltin's Movie and Video Guide 1994, by Leonard Maltin. Signet Books, 1993.

Make It Again, Sam: A Survey of Movie

Remakes, by Michael B. Druxman. A. S. Barnes & Co., 1975.

Making a Monster, by Al Taylor and Sue Roy. Crown Publishers, 1980.

MGM Story, The, by John Douglas Eames. Crown Publishers, 1982.

Movies Made for Television: The Telefeature and the Mini-Series 1964–1986, by Alvin H. Marill. New York Zoetrope, 1987.

Of Mice and Magic: A History of American Animated Cartoons, by Leonard Maltin (revised and updated edition). Plume books, New American Library, 1987.

Parade's Gone By, The, by Kevin Brownlow. Ballantine Books, 1968.

Reel Facts: The Movie Book of Records, by Cobbett Steinberg. Vintage Books, 1980.

Reference Guide to Fantastic Films: Science Fiction, Fantasy and Horror, vol. 1, by Walt Lee. Chelsea-Lee Books, 1972.

Revenge of the Creature Features Movie Guide, 3rd ed., by John Stanley. Creatures at Large Press, 1988.

Science Fiction, Horror and Fantasy Film and Television Credits Supplement: Through 1987, compiled by Harris M. Lentz, III. McFarland & Company, 1989.

Video Source Book, The, edited by David J. Weiner. Gale Research, 1988.

Words on Cassette/Books on Tape. R. R. Bowker, 1992.

Newspapers and Periodicals

"Albert Finney Triumphs as a Musical Scrooge," by Clyde Gilmour. *Toronto Telegram,* November 21, 1970.

"A Christmas Carol," by John Canemaker. *Film News,* September–October, 1971.

"A Christmas Carol," by Aleene MacMinn. *Los Angeles TV Times,* December 19, 1971.

"Christmas in Film," by Allen J. Wiener. *People,* December 6, 1993.

"Holiday Evergreens We Never Grow Tired Of," by Kenneth Turan. *TV Guide,* December 16, 1989.

"Notes in Carol," by Morton Moss. *Los Angeles Herald Examiner.* December 19, 1971.

CHAPTER NINETEEN
CAROLS ON TAPE

HOW AND WHERE TO ORDER
A CHRISTMAS CAROL

Short of haunting your local video store or pawing through your film-buff neighbor's basement, the easiest way to find the various *Christmas Carol* videotapes listed in this book is to buy (or rent) them from a reputable mail-order company.

The following is a short list of companies which not only will probably have that particular tape you're interested in, but are also businesses which Ye Author has personally dealt with in the past.

Names, addresses, phone numbers, and types of tapes favored by the company in question are listed in each entry. Consumers should note that many of these outfits offer extensive catalogs of their inventory, either for free or for a small fee. My advice is, it's always better to know what you want—and how much it's going to

set you back—before ordering anything.

Those interested in purchasing still photographs from various *Carols* should consult the "Still List" immediately following "Carols on Videotape." Those interested in audiotape *Carols* should consult the "Audiotapes" section.

Carols on Videotape

Barr Entertainment
P.O. Box 7878
Irwindale, CA 91706-7878
800-288-7798
    Specializes in mainstream titles, mostly public domain ones.

Captain Bijou
P.O. Box 87
Toney, AL 35773
205-852-0198
    Specializes in B-movies and animation.

Cinema Classics
P.O. Box 174
Village Station
New York, NY 10014
212-675-6692
    "For movie fans by movie fans."

Dickens Video by Mail
5764 Antelope Road
Sacramento, CA 95842
    Specialists in genre films, includes video search service.

Discount Video Tapes
P.O. Box 7122
Burbank, CA 91510
818-843-3366
    "Specializing in the rare and unusual."

Eddie Brandt's Saturday Matinee
6310 Colfax Ave.
N. Hollywood, CA 91606
818-506-4242
    Rents and sells many rare tapes. This is the store Ye Author used as his primary rental source for many of the tapes listed herein. You'll find just about every *Carol*

at Eddie Brandt's; the company also offers a wide selection of stills.

Facets Video
1517 W. Fullerton Ave.
Chicago, IL 60614
800-331-6197 (orders);
312-281-9075 (customer service)
Large inventory, many genres—a mail-order institution.

Foothill Video
P.O. Box 547
Tujunga, CA 91043
818-353-8591
Has large inventory of foreign and silent films.

International Film & Video Center
991 First Ave.
New York, NY 10022
212-826-8848
Rents and sells tapes from the world over; huge inventory.

Movies Unlimited
6736 Castor Ave.
Philadelphia, PA 19149
800-523-0823 (orders),
215-722-8398 (customer service)
America's largest mail-order video dealer; over 30,000 titles!

Video Specialists International
182 Jackson Street
Dallas, PA 18612
717-675-0227
Older but not forgettable films include the Basil Rathbone and Alastair Sim *Carols*.

Video Yesteryear
Box C
Sandy Hook, CT 06482
800-243-0987, 203-426-2574
"The largest manufacturer of quality vintage video in the world."

Whole Toon Catalog
P.O. Box 369, Dept LM
Issaquah, WA 98027
206-391-8747
The company to approach for *Mr. Magoo's Christmas Carol, Alvin's Christmas Carol,* or *Mickey's Christmas*

Carol. Incredible all-animation inventory as well.

Audiotapes

Jimmy B.'s Audio Books
5225 W. Rosecrans Ave.
Hawthorne, CA 90250
310-643-7640
Wide and varied selection of books on tape. Has the Patrick Stewart *Christmas Carol* tape and CD.

Stills List

Collector's Bookstore
1708 N. Vine Street
Hollywood, CA 90028
213-467-3296
Large inventory of animation and live-action *Carol* photographs; also an unusually large number of stills from the 1938 MGM version.

Eddie Brandt's Saturday Matinee

6310 Colfax Avenue
N. Hollywood, CA 91606
818-506-4242
Once again, *the* place to go for your still photograph needs. Has a good selection of photos from the 1938, Alastair Sim and Bill Murray *Carols* in particular.

Hollywood Book and Poster
6349 Hollywood Boulevard
Hollywood, CA 90028
213-465-8764
Eclectic, esoteric, and very helpful; inventory includes photos from the George C. Scott *Carol.*

Larry Edmunds Bookshop, Inc.
6644 Hollywood Boulevard
Hollywood, CA 90028
213-463-3273
"World-wide mail order" from this venerable institution, which was the only store in Hollywood to stock a pressbook of the 1935 *Scrooge.* Many, many stills as well.

CHAPTER TWENTY
THE ANSWERS

Trivia question answers are organized according to the specific chapter and/or adaptation to which they refer.

Chapter One: The Author

1. February 7, 1812.
2. Outside Portsmouth, England.
3. The thuggish Bill Sikes, who murders Oliver's friend Nancy.
4. c. Oliver Reed–*Oliver*!
5. Labeling bottles of boot blacking.
6. Twelve.

7. a. 1859–1861
8. Marshalsea Prison, in London.
9. Miss Haversham, who lives in a decaying mansion and keeps one room dedicated to preserving the wedding feast she never had.
10. Alfred Allen Dickens, who died from "water on the brain."
11. c. *The Pickwick Papers*

12. The Seven Dials (don't you love that name?), a lowlife, slumridden area teeming with pubs, prostitutes, and gamblers. Dickens may have only been a child when he first saw this area, but he never forgot it.
13. d. Elizabeth.
14. An independent shorthand/court reporter. Dickens did this journalistic work at the Doctors Commons, two London quadrangles which contained a series of different courts, including the Admiralty Court.
15. *The Cricket on the Hearth* is one Dickens Christmas story. A Christmas essay was "The Christmas Tree" (1850), wherein the author nostalgically described the toys and joys of his youth.
16. *Morning Chronicle.*
17. Debts incurred by John Dickens, his father. Or you could take the easy way out and just say, "Money."
18. Nell Trent (better known as "Little Nell").
19. 1946. David Lean, who also directed a terrific version of *Oliver Twist* (1948) and other gems before moving on to big-

budget spectacles like *The Bridge on the River Kwai, Lawrence of Arabia,* and *Dr. Zhivago.*
20. Poverty (or lack of money).
21. b. Sydney Carton. All the other names in this question are actual characters from the book, by the way. Except for "Malcolm DeFarge"; *Madame* DeFarge was the vengeful woman who put an entire family to peril in Dickens's classic tale of the French Revolution.
22. b. *Martin Chuzzlewitt,* and e. *American Notes.* Neither book sold very well.
23. "On the ground," a reference to where Dickens wanted to lay after suffering a fit at his dining table.
24. In the dining room of Gad's Hill Place, in Rochester, England. Dickens's father had pointed this stately home out to the young Charles as a place where an ambitious, successful man would live.
25. Six or seven shillings a week, the rough equivalent in American cash of thirty to thirty-five cents.
26. *The Mystery of Edwin Drood.* This novel of a split-personality—seemingly

respectable, opium-smoking murderer—is almost a horror story. But since it was never finished, *Drood* has intrigued Dickens scholars since the day of its author's death, inspiring a number of other creative types to try and come up with their own conclusions. For instance, in 1935 a solid film adaptation starring Claude Rains was produced. And *The Mystery of Edwin Drood* was transformed in the 1980s into a hit Broadway musical! A new filming of the Dickens tale was released in 1994.

27. Dickens is buried in Westminster Abbey, near the House of Parliament and Big Ben. Westminster is the final resting place of many famous English poets, politicians, and heroes.

Chapter Two: The Story

1. December 19, 1843. *A Christmas Carol* was first published by the English firm of Chapman and Hall; Dickens himself went to great pains to ensure that the publisher present his story with the best possible appearance.

2. b. 1846.

3. Time to break out the calculators and calenders here. If *A Christmas Carol* was first published on December 19, 1843, and it took about six weeks from the moment the writing began to the day the book was published, then we have to move *back* forty-two days from December 19. Which makes the answer somewhere around November 8, 1843.

4. "God bless us every one!"

5. Here are four: Scrooge's miserliness is based on Dickens's own obsession with money; "Tiny Tim" was partly derived from a nickname for Dickens's brother Frederick, who was called "Tiny Fred"; the physical description of Bob Cratchit's house was based on the Dickens family's first home in London; both Scrooge and Dickens were taken from school at a young age and forced to work in factories. There are other real-life influences in *A Christmas Carol*—see if you can come up with some more.

6. d. 32.

7. The illustrator for the first edition of *A Christmas Carol* was the rather alarm-

ingly named Mr. John Leech; cost of the book was five shillings, or about twenty-five cents.

8. Besides enriching our popular culture with one heck of a story, the biggest change is the manner in which Dickens's tale helped shift the emphasis on Christmas away from a quiet, family-oriented day to a festive holiday *season* emphasizing good will to everyone.

9. In a glass case at New York's Pierpont Morgan Library.

10. "Merry Christmas, humbug!"

11. *Martin Chuzzlewitt* and *The Pickwick Papers.* From the former, Dickens recycled the themes of selfishness and greed; in the latter, the idea of supernatural beings showing an old man the past and future.

12. Rochester, in the county of Kent. You really should try to visit the town any weekend in December.

13. The Bible.

14. c.   6,000 copies—five days.

15. Benjamin Disraeli, who left us this notable quote: "There are lies, damn lies,

and statistics."

16. Sleeplessness, long nocturnal walks, talking, laughing and crying to himself, and generally carrying on like a New York City street person.

17. Dickens first thought up *A Christmas Carol* during a journey to Manchester, where he was to give a speech at the Manchester Athenaeum, a charitable center for that city's working class. Incidentally, one of the directors of this center was none other than Dickens's sister Frances Elizabeth—better known as "Fanny."

18. For money, and to use the story as a tool for social change (i.e., the education of poor children).

19. Jacob Marley. His supernatural penance is to carry a long chain of cash boxes wrapped around and trailing behind his body throughout eternity. And the way he frightens Scrooge is by unwinding the burial cloth wrapped under his neck so that his jaw drops down.

20. Scrooge is a moneylender.

21. Dickens's first public reading of *A*

Christmas Carol took place December 27, 1854. His last occurred March 15, 1870.

22. 450.
23. Tickets to Dickens's first public reading in America cost two dollars. This reading took place in 1865 in Boston.
24. Three hours.
25. The pirated *Carol* added songs(!).

Chapter Three: The Best Version

1. Sim was thirty before he began to act. Originally, he was a teacher of phonetics and elocution.
2. The answer to this one requires a careful examination of the credits on both adaptations. Only one name appears on both films: Clive Donner, who worked as film editor on the 1951 Alastair Sim version and as director of the 1984, made-for-TV *A Christmas Carol*, which starred George C. Scott.
3. *Scrooge.*
4. There are at least three other titles visible on the bookshelf. All are by Dickens: *Great Expectations, The Pickwick Papers,* and *Oliver Twist.*
5. Alastair Sim not only played Scrooge in the classic 1951 version but also provided the *voice* of Ebenezer in the superb, animated-short version of *A Christmas Carol* in 1971. Michael Hordern, who appeared as Marley in the 1951 version, also supplied Marley's voice for the 1971 cartoon.
6. The song heard over the opening credits is "Hark! The Herald Angels Sing," which also ran over the main titles for the 1935 *Scrooge.*
7. The words are: "*A Christmas Carol*–Stave 1–Marley's Ghost."
8. At the London Exchange, a mercantile center for stocks and bartering.
9. Help Scrooge remove his hat, coat, gloves, and muffler.
10. Scrooge arrives at his office promptly at five P.M. You can see a clock on the wall near Cratchit's desk (it's also tolling the hour).
11. "If they would rather die, they had better do it, and decrease the surplus popula-

tion." This classic line is found in almost every version of the story.

12. A Christmas goose.

13. Scrooge asks for more bread while eating dinner in the tavern. He decides not to get it because it would cost him an extra half-penny.

14. As he's going up his shadowy staircase, Ebenezer hears his own name whispered in the dark: "Scrooogggge . . ."

15. Marley's Ghost appears a few minutes past ten P.M. You can see this time on a clock in Scrooge's living room.

16. Eighteen years. We find this out during the Ghost of Christmas Past sequence; the Past Ghost mentions the duration Scrooge and Marley worked together during that shot where Scrooge signs the register of Marley's burial.

17. "Much."

18. When Marley's Ghost asks Scrooge why he doesn't believe in him, the latter replies, "You might be an undigested bit of beef. A piece of cheese. A fragment of an underdone potato. There's more of gravy than of grave in you." For fun, you might want to keep these lines in the back of your head, just to see how often they turn up in *other* versions of *A Christmas Carol.*

19. Scrooge sees a poor woman sitting in the snow with her baby, surrounded by dozens of moaning, gesticulating ghosts (called "Wandering Spirits").

20. One A.M.

21. Scrooge says he's afraid to go out the window because "I am mortal, and may fall!"

22. Scrooge's sister's name is Fran. When she runs to greet the young Ebenezer, she runs *straight through* the ghostly form of Alastair Sim—a nice touch not found in any other version. And the sweet, traditional ballad which plays over this scene is called "Barbara Allen."

23. An apprentice clerk.

24. Scrooge's fiancée is named Alice in this version—an odd choice for a film that's otherwise so faithful to its source material (many other adaptations call her "Belle").

25. The initial of Fezziwig's first name is "S."

You can see it painted on his office door during that scene when he's first visited by the businessman, Mr. Jorkin, who's come with an offer to buy Fezziwig out.

26. Patrick Macnee–who later went on to stardom playing the suave, bowler-hatted secret agent John Steed, of *The Avengers*–portrays the young Jacob Marley.

27. After the young Scrooge first goes to work for Mr. Jorkin, there's a scene where we see a mournful Mr. Fezziwig sitting in a carriage on the street. Fezziwig's watching two men remove his business sign from the outside of a building. And if you freeze-frame your VCR, you'll see that that sign reads "A.D. 1766, Merchants, Shippers and Warehouseman"–the year Fezziwig's business was established, plus the exact nature of that business!

28. Jorkin's company was named "The Amalgamated Mercantile Society." You find this out during the scene where the company officials have a meeting to discuss the fact that Jorkin is an embezzler.

29. Touch the robe of the Ghost.

30. Bob carries Tiny Tim home on his shoulder.

31. Gin punch(!).

32. Ignorance.

33. The Ghost of Christmas Yet-to-Come is an eerie figure draped in a coal-black sheet. It doesn't talk, and you never see its face. You *do* see its (human) pointing hand, though.

34. The charwoman, laundress, and undertaker meet at "Joe's Shop." The undertaker sells Scrooge's "Watch, fob, pencil case, seal, sleeve buttons, and brooch."

35. "Are these the shadows of things that must be, or shadows of things that might be?"–yet another oft-quoted line.

36. This was a trick question, since no date of death is inscribed on Scrooge's tombstone. However, *other* versions of the story *do* show Scrooge's date of death. And some of them are different! So keep your eyes peeled.

37. During the Christmas morning scene in Scrooge's bedroom, Alastair Sim runs to a small mirror hanging over the wash

basin. He looks into that mirror twice. Both times, you can see the reflection of an unwary film-crew member (wearing modern clothing) peeking around the curtains behind Sim's back, and staring at the camera!

38. The Cratchits live at "2 Porter Street, Camden Town." This is the address on the card which Scrooge sends with the Christmas turkey to the Cratchit home.
39. A coal-scuttle.
40. "Uncle Scrooge!"

Chapter Four: Recommended Film Versions

Scrooge (aka *A Christmas Carol*) (1935)

1. "Hark! The Herald Angels Sing."
2. "I have endeavoured in this Ghostly little book to raise the Ghost of an Idea which shall not put my readers out of humour with themselves, with each other, with the season, or with me. May it haunt their houses pleasantly, and no one wish to lay it." And if you could actually *quote* all that, from memory, you owe yourself

a glass of eggnog!
3. "A round half-dozen" children—"three boys and three girls."
4. "Because I fell in love."
5. The mayor of London. He toasts the Queen.
6. What's different about Marley's Ghost in this version is that *the audience never sees him!* Yes, Marley's *face* does (briefly) appear on Scrooge's doorknocker. But during his entire scene in Scrooge's rooms, Marley's *Ghost* remains invisible. Only Ebenezer can see him (which is certainly one way to cut down on a special effects budget!).
7. At the stroke of midnight.
8. The "poor man" is played by Maurice Evans, who later went on to a distinguished stage career and to portray key film roles in *Rosemary's Baby* (as the old friend who first alerts Mia Farrow that she's living in an apartment building filled with witches) and *Planet of the Apes* (where he was transformed by makeup artist John Chambers into a talking orangutan named Dr. Zaius).

9. Belle.
10. The Ghost of Christmas Present says he has "more than 1800" brothers.
11. By carrying him on his back.
12. Mrs. Cratchit describes Scrooge as "an odious, stingy, hard, unfeeling man."
13. "Hark! The Herald Angels Sing." Again (see the 1951 *Carol*!).
14. Scrooge's laundress steals his nightshirt by taking it off Ebenezer's dead body.
15. The Ghost of Christmas Yet-to-Come is mostly the shadow of a pointing hand. And no, you never see its face.
16. Cratchit says, "I was making rather merry yesterday."
17. Scrooge's final line is "God bless us, every one"—with apologies to Tiny Tim.

A Christmas Carol (1938)

1. The words "Ars Gratia Artis" on MGM's logo mean—roughly—"Art for art's sake."
2. "Humbug!"
3. Tiny Tim (Terry Kilburn) is watching a group of children slide down an icy street on their feet—he can't join them, of course, because of his crippled leg.

Scrooge's kindhearted nephew Fred (Barry Mackay) then hoists Tim onto his back, and *both* of them slide down the street!

4. A bottle of wine. Port wine.
5. Cough medicine.
6. Fifteen shillings six pence (or "15 and 6," as it's phrased in the dialogue). The way this sum is determined all revolves around the scene where Cratchit unwittingly ruins Scrooge's hat. If you listen carefully, an angry Ebenezer informs Cratchit that a new hat will cost Scrooge "16 and 6—exactly one shilling more per week than I pay you."
7. Because Bob unwittingly knocks Ebenezer's hat off the miser's head with a snowball—a hat that's run over by a carriage, ruined, and the cause of the conversation in answer number 6!
8. "God Rest Ye Merry Gentlemen."
9. Moments after Marley's Ghost enters Scrooge's room, a town herald can be heard yelling the time outside Ebenezer's window—ten P.M. As for the Ghost of Christmas Yet-to-Come, this

eerie spirit visits Scrooge in the dead of night–three A.M.

10. Joseph L. Mankiewicz became a noted writer-director in the 1940s. Among his more famous efforts were such classics as *The Ghost and Mrs. Muir* (1947), *Julius Caesar* (1953), *Guys and Dolls* (1955), *Suddenly Last Summer* (1959), and *Sleuth* (1972). Mankiewicz was also unfortunate enough to have directed 1963's notorious megabomb *Cleopatra* starring Elizabeth Taylor. In 1949, Mankiewicz won Oscars for writing and directing *A Letter to Three Wives*. He repeated this double feat the following year with the witty, bitchy *All About Eve* which also won the Best Picture Oscar that year.

11. Fezziwig gives the young Scrooge a gold sovereign.

12. He has "some 1800" brothers–or approximately one brother for every year since the time of Christ's birth (up to the time of *A Christmas Carol*).

13. Here's a chance to use the "Still" button on your VCR. If you freeze-frame the scene taking place outside the "John Falderton Bakery"–the establishment where the Ghost of Christmas Present tells Scrooge the poor take their Christmas dinners to be cooked–you'll see a sign on the bakery's wall, one that begins with the words "Save Your Pennies." Now, look at the *bottom* of that sign. You'll discover that a pre-cooked Christmas dinner costs exactly . . . six cents!

14. "The spirit of Christmas Cheer, five times distilled."

15. Composer Franz Waxman provided the musical score for both MGM's *A Christmas Carol* and Universal's *Bride of Frankenstein*.

16. "Aladdin and the Magic Lamp."

17. Prince Albert introduced the Christmas tree into England. The first tree in London was set up in Windsor Castle in 1840.

18. Freeze-frame time again. If you hit the Pause button on your VCR during the scene where the Ghost of Christmas Yet-to-Come shows Scrooge his own tomb-

stone, you'll be able to see the year this unrepentant Scrooge died—1845.

19. A miniature musical Merry-Go-Round.

20. Leo G. Carroll had already appeared (on stage and screen) as every male character mentioned in *A Christmas Carol* before he acted in MGM's version. And for the 1938 film, this gentle, jowled character actor played the part of Marley's Ghost.

21. The Ghost of Christmas Yet-to-Come—who makes his entrance on a barren, windswept hill dotted by leafless trees, a set that looks like it was carted over from a Universal *Frankenstein* movie—wears the black robes of a hooded monk. And you never do really see its face, although there are flashes of a human actor's features visible inside its cowl during some of the long shots. Also, when the Ghost points to the Cratchit's window outside their house, you get to see a very normal hand and forearm.

22. Belinda Cratchit. June Lockhart got sick from having to eat a rum-and-salt-soaked English pudding. More than once.

Chapter Five: The Silent Film Versions

1. The earliest known silent film version of *A Christmas Carol* was released in 1901. It was produced in England.

2. *The Right to Be Happy* (1916), which starred Rupert Julian as Scrooge, was criticized for being filmed in sunny Southern California.

3. Two silent Italian film versions of *A Christmas Carol* (although they may possibly be reedited versions of the same film) were *The Dream of Old Scrooge* and *Old Scrooge*. Both were released in 1910.

4. *Scrooge* starring and written by Sir Seymour Hicks, was released in 1913.

5. Charlie Chaplin.

6. The world's first film studio was built in 1893 by Thomas Edison. It was called "The Black Maria."

7. Ten.

Chapter Six: The Best Made-for-TV Version

A Christmas Carol (1984)

1. It premiered on the CBS television network the night of December 17, 1984. A Monday.
2. To practice his craft and to have fun.
3. The George C. Scott version was filmed on location in the town of Shrewsbury, England.
4. The two events which irrevocably soured Scrooge were his father's hatred of the young Ebenezer and the breakup of the latter's engagement to his sweetheart, because he chose money over love. *Vive le Freud!*
5. Silas Scrooge, Ebenezer's father, was played by Nigel Davenport. In 1965, Davenport was the pilot of a small aircraft in the British survival film *Sands of the Kalahari*. Forced to crash-land in the desert, Davenport and a few other survivors then had to battle with a tribe of vicious baboons over the only water hole. In 1974, Davenport played a scientist matching wits with alarmingly intelligent ants in the sci-fi cult hit *Phase IV*.
6. Surprise! Anthony Walters, who played Tiny Tim, had appeared in *no* other pictures, British or otherwise, prior to *A Christmas Carol*. This TV-movie was Walters's motion picture debut—a fact underlined by his credit on the film, which reads, "Introducing Anthony Walters as Tiny Tim."
7. Edward Woodward (who later became a TV star as *The Equalizer*) stands 5'10" tall. In order to gain the 7'6" height of the Ghost of Christmas Present, Woodward was strapped into metal stilts. And the thing he hated most about playing this Ghost was having to wear a chest wig.
8. The corporation which both sponsored and helped cofinance this *Carol* was IBM—otherwise known as *International Business Machines*.
9. Susannah York played Mrs. Cratchit; two of her real-life children—Sasha, who was eleven at the time, and Orlando, who was ten—played two of Mrs. Cratchit's kids.

10. The four-part eight-hour *Masada* (1981), which concerned a celebrated event in Jewish history, in which nine hundred Zealots in a mountaintop fortress heroically withstood the repeated assaults of five thousand Roman soldiers. Warner played the part of Pomponious Falco, a devious Roman commander.

11. Nick Bicat.

12. The Christopher Award for Distinguished Achievement in Television. Founded in 1945 by the Rev. James Keller, the Christophers are an ecumenical organization whose credo is "Better to light one candle than to curse the darkness." The awards honor those radio and television programs that "affirm the highest values of the human spirit, exhibit artistic and technical proficiency, and attain a significant degree of public acceptance."

13. *Dr. Strangelove*, in which Scott played the rabidly right-wing Gen. Buck Turgidson, who, after being told that a nuclear war with the Russians would destroy the planet, replied, "I'm not saying we wouldn't get our hair mussed a little."

14. Scott actually suggested at least three books in the "Read All About It" segment which the Library of Congress felt would better acquaint the viewer with the worlds of Charles Dickens and Christmas: *A Christmas Carol* by Charles Dickens (naturally), *Charles Dickens, His Tragedy and Triumph* and *Christmas Customs Around the World*, by Herbert H. Wernecke.

Chapter Seven: Other Television Versions

1. The earliest television *Carol* listed in this book was titled *Christmas Carol*. It was broadcast from television station WBKB, in Chicago, during the month of December 1945.

2. *The General Electric Theater* (hosted by future President and economy-wrecker Ronald Reagan) broadcast "The Trail to Christmas" in 1957. This "cowboy *Carol*" featured an appearance by James Stewart, who also directed.

An American Christmas Carol

3. Although it's supposed to take place in 1933 in the small town of Concord, New Hampshire, *An American Christmas Carol* was actually filmed outside Toronto. Maybe the producers should have titled this "A *North* American Christmas Carol"!

4. The Ebenezer Scrooge-like character here, played by Henry Winkler, is named Benedict Slade.

5. A pamphlet on the lives of self-made men like Calvin Coolidge and J. Pierpoint Morgan.

6. "Claptrap!"

7. Slade prompts the visit of his dead partner by ripping out some pages from a first edition of *A Christmas Carol.*

8. A furniture manufacturing plant.

9. "S & L—Slade & Latham."

10. The full name of the Tiny Tim surrogate is Jonathan Thatcher. His father's nickname for him is "My little Mr. T." The boy has polio.

11. The Ghost of Christmas Yet-to-Come—who here is called "The Spirit of Christmas Future"—is played by black actor Dorian Harewood, dressed in a seventies-style black suit, complete with a wide white collar and gold chains hung around his neck. He most definitely speaks.

12. Rick Baker, who won an Academy Award for his makeup work on *An American Werewolf in London* and *Harry and the Hendersons,* did Winkler's Benedict Slade makeup as well.

Carol for Another Christmas

13. Rod Serling, better known for creating *The Twilight Zone,* wrote the teleplay for this program.

14. The danger facing the world was nuclear annihilation from H-bombs.

15. Sterling Hayden played the Scrooge clone. His character's name was Daniel Grudge.

George Burns Comedy Week

16. James Whitmore played Scrooge, Ed Begley Jr. was Tiny Tim.

John Grin's Christmas

17. Robert Guillaume, star of the television comedy series *Soap* and *Benson*, played the Scrooge-like toymaker John Grin.
18. This *Christmas Carol* is unusual because it was played by black actors.

Rich Little's Christmas Carol

19. W. C. Fields.
20. The W. C. Fields/Scrooge character is in "The boat and bottle business": Fields empties the bottles, and his assistant (Little as Bob Cratchit/Paul Lynde) builds miniature ships in them. The answer "Ship in a bottle" business is also acceptable.
21. Richard M. Nixon plays Marley's Ghost. He's wrapped up in spools of audiotape, a reference to the Watergate Tapes (and this version's only witty touch).
22. A waterbed filled with beer.
23. Truman Capote.
24. For the Ghost of Christmas Yet-to-Come, Little impersonates Peter Sellers playing the bumbling Inspector Clouseau. And yes, he does speak—with a bad French accent.

"The Spirit of Christmas"

25. William Lundigan (who also starred in the fifties TV series *Men Into Space*) was the host for CBS's *Shower of Stars,* on which "The Spirit of Christmas" first aired.
26. "The Spirit of Christmas" was originally broadcast in color, although videocassettes of this program are in black-and-white.
27. Plymouth, DeSoto, Dodge, and Chrysler cars are promoted on the show. Plus "the exclusive Imperial!"
28. The exhaustively cheerful Ray Middleton.
29. Bernard Herrman (it's pronounced HER-men, not her-MON) did the music for this show. His first film score was for *Citizen Kane* (and a marvelous score it is!).
30. Basil Rathbone was born in 1982 in Johannesburg, South Africa. He died in 1967.
31. Marley's Ghost removes Scrooge & Marley's old business ledger from his chains, which is a record of "thousands of injustices."
32. Scrooge trips over the business ledger,

which Marley leaves after he vanishes.

33. March won a Best Actor Award in 1932 for portraying *Dr. Jekyll and Mr. Hyde*. The cowinner that year was Wallace Beery, for *The Champ*.

34. The Ghost of Christmas Present takes off Scrooge's nightcap and kisses the old man on the scalp (!).

35. A mynah bird sitting in a tree! And no, it doesn't talk. Even if it is a mynah bird.

36. 1843.

37. From a Christmas wreath hanging on an office across the street.

38. "Barbie."

39. The photograph on the front of the cassette box *isn't* from the enclosed Fredric March tape, but from the 1956 musical *Alcoa Hour* version–which starred Basil Rathbone as Scrooge and Martyn Green as Cratchit!

Chapter Eight: The Big-Budget Musical Version

1. Ronald Searle, a British artist who was somewhat in vogue during the late six-ties–early seventies.

2. Leslie Bricusse (pronounced BRICK-us) wrote the screenplay *and* composed the score (words and music) for *Scrooge*.

3. Despite the fact that *Scrooge* is an original musical, the first song we hear after the credits is . . . "Hark! the Herald Angels Sing." The same hymn also opens both the Seymour Hicks and Alastair Sim versions of *A Christmas Carol*.

4. Nephew Fred comes to visit at a couple of minutes before seven P.M. The time is clearly seen on a clock in Scrooge's office.

5. Cratchit tells his children he has fifteen shillings in his pocket; apples are six for a penny.

6. Exactly seven years to the day at the start of *Scrooge*–a period which is the same in virtually every other adaptation.

7. The makeup to change Albert Finney into *Scrooge* took two hours a day to apply.

8. A fireplace poker.

9. Nothing. Although a chair slides magically sideways toward Marley without being

touched, the Ghost then sits down on—thin air!

10. "Because I couldn't do it!"

11. Isabel. This is the only such time she's called that in a filmed adaptation. And after she tosses her engagement ring on Scrooge's money-weighing scale, the ring is then outweighed by a pile of coins—a nice way of visualizing Scrooge's choice of money over love.

12. 1860, seventeen years after *A Christmas Carol* was first published. This date is mentioned when the Ghost of Christmas Present and Scrooge first meet.

13. The Present Ghost says he has "1859" brothers.

14. The Milk of Human Kindness.

15. The main course of the Cratchit's Christmas dinner is "Roast goose with sage and onion stuffing."

16. Initially, the Ghost of Christmas Yet-to-Come is fairly traditional—dark robes and cowl, with no face. It doesn't speak. But just toward the end of the film, when he causes Scrooge to fall into his open grave, you *do* see the Future Ghost's

face. It looks something like a green plastic skull.

17. Paddy Stone, who was *Scrooge's* choreographer, also played the Ghost of Christmas Yet-to-Come.

18. Tom Jenkins—who is one of Scrooge's debtors—leads the crowd in singing "Thank You Very Much" to celebrate Ebenezer's death. Tom runs a foodstall as his business.

19. Lucifer wants Ebenezer to be his personal clerk—in Hell.

20. A "Father Christmas" costume, the English equivalent of our own Santa Claus.

21. Father Christmas's beard and hat.

22. Rex Harrison—who talked to the animals in *Doctor Dolittle*—had been approached to play *Scrooge*.

Chapter Nine: The Funniest Version

1. Blackadder runs a "Moustache Shop" located in "Old Dumpling Lane."

2. Baldrick is forced to substitute a dog for Baby Jesus, since the infant who was

originally going to play the part died.

3. Rowan Atkinson.
4. Mrs. Scratchit and Tiny Tom.
5. God.
6. By knocking down the door.
7. Edmund Blackadder.
8. Miranda Richardson. The same actress—whose sendup of Queen Elizabeth during the regular 1989 series run of *Blackadder* endeared her to British television audiences—portrayed doomed murderess Ruth Ellis in the English film *Dance With a Stranger* (1985) and a ruthless IRA assassin in the gender-bending art-house hit *The Crying Game* (1992).
9. A scanty leather loincloth.
10. The Elizabethan Period, the Regency Period, and (as noted on the *Blackadder* videocassette box), the Space Age.
11. The newly mean Blackadder describes his niece as being "blessed with a head that's emptier than a hermit's address book."
12. They disguise themselves as commoners and wander the London streets dressed

like ordinary folks.

13. A baronet and 50,000 pounds.
14. "Queen piglet features."
15. The wishbone. With no meat on it.

Chapter Ten: The Best Musical Version

1. Although at least four or five people could be said to have helped in the creation of Mr. Magoo—including writer Millard Kaufman, who wrote the story for *Ragtime Bear*, the first Magoo cartoon—the general consensus is that it was producer-director-animator John Hubley who had the strongest creative input into the character's genesis.
2. Jule Styne (who did the music) and Bob Merrill (the lyrics).
3. "Show-News"
4. No. He gets to the theater half an hour late.
5. Jim Backus played tormented James Dean's weak, apron-wearing father in *Rebel Without A Cause*. As for *Gilligan's Island*, the character Backus played was filthy rich Thurston Howell III.

6. Magoo first sings "Ringle, Ringle" in his office as he's counting his money.
7. Magoo wipes away Marley's ghostly face from the doorknocker with his handkerchief. He then says, "Very strange—could I need spectacles?" A blatantly self-referential joke, since Magoo's famous for his nearsightedness!
8. "That sour gruel I had for supper."
9. Marley's Ghost appears at midnight. The time is clearly visible on the clock on Magoo's endtable.
10. The difference here regarding the three Christmas Ghosts is actually a major one. For only in *Mr. Magoo's Christmas Carol* is the Ghost of Christmas Present the first Ghost to appear! Followed by the Ghosts of Christmas Past and Future.
11. Tiny Tim is played by Gerald McBoing Boing, an endearing UPA character who usually spoke in sound effects. Or simply said "Boing, Boing" instead. But in *Magoo's Carol*, Gerald *talks*. And sings.
12. Tim's favorite food is "Razzleberry dressing." His second favorite is "Woffeljelly cake."
13. The chorus to "All Alone in the World" goes like this:
A hand for each hand was planned for the world
Why don't my fingers reach?
Millions of grains of sand in the world
Why such a lonely beach?
Where is a voice to answer mine back?
Where are two shoes that click to my clack?
I'm all alone in the world . . .
14. A spring of holly which it waves like a magic wand.
15. The big bright flame which burns on top of its head gets smaller and dimmer.
16. In this version, the Ghost of Christmas Yet-to-Come is known as "The Ghost of the Future." It's a *red*-robed phantom, which flutters beside Magoo like a rag in the wind . . . and no, you never see its face.
17. James, Brady, and Billings.
18. The undertaker steals Magoo's boots and cuff buttons, which he sells at "Ye Olde Junk Shoppe," clearly indicated by a sign hanging outside the building.

19. Four, counting Tiny Tim.
20. Another trick question–*nobody* plays nephew Fred in this version. In fact, the character doesn't even appear in *Mr. Magoo's Christmas Carol*!
21. In this version, the Cratchits live at "21 Groveny Lane."
22. By himself in a graveyard.
23. "A shining star of Christmas gold."
24. *Magoo's Carol* was released theatrically in 1970, as part of a "kiddie matinee" double-feature, on a bill with *Mr. Magoo's Little Snow White*.
25. "Merry Christmas, everyone!"

Chapter Eleven: The Best Animated Version

1. Richard Williams's version of *A Christmas Carol* begins exactly at three P.M.—you can clearly see this on the large clock which serves as a background graphic for Williams's directorial credit.
2. A lion.
3. The supernatural shape which passes Scrooge on his staircase is a ghostly, horse-drawn hearse.
4. Marley convinces Scrooge he's really dead by untying the bandage from around his head—with the result that his jaw immediately, and alarmingly, drops down past his chest, opening his mouth in an impossibly wide grimace. This ghastly detail is from Dickens's original story, by the way, but has rarely been used in the various adaptations—a detail based on the old English custom of tying a cloth under a corpse's jaw to keep its mouth shut after death.
5. There are only three pieces—two chairs and an endtable. Otherwise, the large room is completely bare.
6. The night sky, filled with moaning phantoms.
7. Fezziwig celebrates Christmas by throwing a party for all his employees—one complete with feasting, dancing, and fiddling.
8. On top of its head is a huge, white candle flame. Another, rarely utilized detail from the original story.
9. The beloved, much repeated holiday clas-

sic, *How the Grinch Stole Christmas*, in 1965 (available on MGM UA Home Video). This Dr. Seuss adaptation starred the voice of Boris Karloff. Chuck Jones's debut as a cartoon director occurred on November 19, 1938 with the Warner Brothers short *The Night Watchman*, a sweet story concerning a young kitten taking over its father's job as a night watchman in a kitchen.

10. In its right hand, a sprig of holly; in its left a giant, conical candle snuffer–the same object Scrooge snatches away and pulls down over the Ghost's head, which snuffs it out like a candle.

11. A leg brace.

12. The Ghost of Christmas Present shows Scrooge a family of miners celebrating Christmas, two lighthouse keepers making merry, and a sailor steering a ship while singing a Christmas hymn.

13. The Jones-Williams version of *A Christmas Carol* took over 30,000 individual drawings to make a twenty-six-minute film.

14. The Spirit of Ignorance is a boy; the Spirit of Want, a girl.

15. Exactly on the stroke of midnight.

16. Scrooge's eyes are blue–a rather *pretty* blue, I might add.

17. Scrooge's former business acquaintances disparagingly refer to him as "Old Scratch"–a nickname for the Devil.

18. It's spelled "Prize Turkee."

19. When Bob Cratchit comes in late for work, a clock on the office wall clearly reads "9:18 A.M." Yet in the next shot Scrooge is seen checking his pocket watch, which just as clearly reads "10:25 A.M."–the only instance of a continuity error in the film.

20. This version, of course–for Best Short Subject, Animated Film, in 1972.

Chapter Twelve: The Disney Version

1. From 1961 to 1966, Alan Young starred on television with a sardonic talking horse named *Mr. Ed*. The actor who supplied Mr. Ed's voice was one-time cowboy star Alan "Rocky" Lane. As for the fantasy film, in 1960 Alan Young appeared in

director-producer George Pal's charming adaptation of the H. G. Wells sci-fi classic *The Time Machine*. He played two characters: David Filby (a red-haired Scotsman who was the best friend of Time Traveler Rod Taylor), and Jamie Filby, David's son. Over the course of the film, Jamie is seen as both a young and very old man!

2. The name "Marley" has been crossed out.

3. To thaw out the ink in a frozen inkwell, which is sitting on the stove.

4. Some sources cite the 1928 sound cartoon titled *Steamboat Willie* as the famous rodent's first screen appearance. They are wrong—*Steamboat Willie* may have been the first *sound* cartoon, but this was actually Mickey's *third* screen appearance. The first Mickey cartoon was titled *Plane Crazy*, a silent film released in early 1928. The second cartoon was also a 1928 silent, titled *Gallopin' Gaucho*.

5. The three men who supplied Mickey's voice up until 1984 were:

a. Walt Disney, who originated the voice.

b. Jimmy MacDonald, who took over the vocal chores in 1947 (for *Mickey and the Beanstalk*).

c. Wayne Allwine spoke for the mouse in *Mickey's Christmas Carol.*

6. Donald—who, after all, is a duck—plans on having a goose for Christmas dinner (!).

7. A Christmas wreath.

8. Clarence "Ducky" Nash supplied the voice of Donald Duck for 128 cartoons (at least until 1983). Donald first appeared in *The Wise Little Hen* (1934).

9. Bernie Mattinson, who started with the Disney organization in 1953 by working in the studio mailroom.

10. "Talk is cheap."

11. McDuck squeezes its nose.

12. "Ghost of Christmas Past—Official."

13. According to *The Making Of Mickey's Christmas Carol*, 118.

14. Mr. Toad, one of the leading characters in Disney's short film *The Wind in the Willows*, is Fezziwig. He plays a fiddle during Fezziwig's Christmas party.

15. Daisy Duck.

16. Daisy was originally called Donna Duck in her first screen appearance.
17. The Giant rips a streetlamp out of the sidewalk and uses it as a flashlight (don't ask Ye Author where he finds the power for it, though!).
18. Scrooge McDuck's laundry.
19. Mark Henn.
20. Under its cowl and robes, the Ghost is a king-size version of a Disney-dog named Black Pete. The thing it does which no other Future Ghosts have done is smoke a cigar.
21. According to *The Making of Mickey's Christmas Carol*, Alan Young and partner Alan Dinehart wrote a comedy version of this story that was released on a Walt Disney record in the late 1970s. This album was titled *Dickens' Christmas Carol: Performed by the Walt Disney Players*. Portions of the Young and Dinehart script for this recording were then used for the screenplay of *Mickey's Christmas Carol*, on which both received a story credit.

Chapter Thirteen: Other Animated Versions

Alvin's Christmas Carol (1983)

1. Alvin's brothers are Theodore and Simon.
2. *The Muppet Christmas Carol.* The Disney organization released both this title and *Alvin's Christmas Carol* on the Disney home video label.
3. David Seville was the stage name for Ross Bagdasarian, who not only created the Chipmunks but also originally provided the voices for Alvin, Theodore, Simon, and Uncle Dave.
4. Alvin's elderly neighbor is called "Mr. Carol"; his cat is named "Ebenezer."
5. Simon is building an "automatic sock sorter"; Theodore is baking gingerbread men.
6. "The True Meaning of Christmas."
7. Alvin Seville.

A Christmas Carol (1969)

8. Just before Marley's arrival, an old fashioned hand bell rises up off Scrooge's

fireplace mantel and, floating in the air, rings itself.

9. "He's so tight-fisted he can't get his gloves off at night."

10. Marley's Ghost has a skull's face and flames burning on its head.

11. "At the three of the clock."

12. The first sovereign he ever made. Incidentally, at the end of the story Scrooge pays for the Cratchit's Christmas turkey with this same sovereign.

A Christmas Carol (1982)

13. One.

14. The doorknocker in this version has no animal's shape whatsoever. It's just a plain, ordinary knocker.

15. Marley's Ghost throws a chair on the fire!

16. Scrooge's fiancée is called both Belle *and* Adela.

17. "Second Hand Wares."

18. The Ghost is a traditional dark-robed and hooded model. You never see its face, and it doesn't speak. But it does have a dark blue human hand.

A Jetsons Christmas Carol (1985)

19. Spacely Space Sprockets, Inc.

20. Cosmo.

21. Elroy Jetson attends the Little Dipper School; Judy goes to Orbit High School.

22. Marsley.

23. The Spirit of Christmas Past—who, incidentally, takes Spacely into a past that's still very much the future—is a giant, disembodied, talking robot head. The Spirit of Christmas Present is exactly that: a huge, talking, gift-wrapped box.

24. A towering, monolithic computer, with blinking lights, no face, no eyes. And no, it doesn't talk. But it beeps.

25. That Astro will die after eating a Spacely Sprocket. The Jetsons will then sue Cosmo for Astro's death and become filthy rich, while Mr. Spacely will become a penniless bum.

26. Judy gets nuclear rocket skates; Elroy, a Rocketbow Guitar.

27. Astro.

28. George O'Hanlon and Penny Singleton were the voices of George and Jane Jetson; Janet Waldo and Daws Butler

vocalized Judy and Elroy. As for Mr. Spacely, his dialogue was spoken by the voice of Mr. Bugs Bunny himself, Mel Blanc.

Chapter Fourteen: The Muppet Version

1. *The Muppet Christmas Carol* is dedicated "In Loving memory of Jim Henson and Richard Hunt." Jim Henson, of course, was the famous creator of the Muppets, who had died a short time before this picture was released. Richard Hunt, on the other hand, was a not-so-famous Henson Productions puppeteer and vocal artist.
2. If you answered "Mrs. Cratchit" here, you're only half right. Miss Piggy's character's full name is *Emily* Cratchit.
3. Himself.
4. Rizzo the Rat is an inversion of the name "Ratso Rizzo," who was portrayed by Dustin Hoffman in *Midnight Cowboy* (1969).
5. Selling apples.
6. Gonzo picks up Rizzo and uses him as a dustrag to wipe off the window.
7. Scrooge picks up the waiting debtor and throws him bodily out of the office.
8. Scrooge's accountants are a bunch of rats. Literally.
9. The Marley brothers are named Jacob and Robert.
10. One A.M.
11. By lassoing a rope around Scrooge's ankle and dangling in the sky from his leg, while Ebenezer flies into the past.
12. Aristotle, Dante, Moliére, and Shakespeare.
13. Singing grapes.
14. The party game's called "Yes and No."
15. Belinda and Bettina.
16. "On the stroke of twelve."
17. Because they're frightened of the Ghost of Christmas Yet-to-Come: "This is too scary!"
18. You never see the Future ghost's face; it's covered by a dark veil within its hood. And this Spirit is portrayed as an eight-foot-tall figure wearing silvery-white robes, with gaunt, human hands sheathed in gray plastic gloves.

19. Another trick question, since the under-taker is played not by an animal, but by an insect—a spider, to be exact.
20. On Christmas morning, Scrooge passes by the two, pauses for a moment, pats Gonzo on the shoulder, and wishes him "A Merry Christmas!"
21. Two buckets of coal.
22. The last bits of dialogue belong to Gonzo and Rizzo:
    Rizzo:"Nice story, Mr. Dickens."
    Gonzo:"Oh, thanks. If you liked this, you should read the book."
    And you should!

Chapter Fifteen: Dance, Spoken-Word, and One-Shot Versions

1. Desmond Davis directed Rathbone as Scrooge in 1962.
2. Fat Albert found himself squaring off against miserly junkyard owner Tightwad Tyrone.
3. *Scrooge's Rock 'n' Roll Christmas*.
4. The Guthrie Theater Company hails from Minneapolis.

5. While commanding the *Enterprise*, Captain Picard likes to relax with a nice hot cup of Earl Grey tea.
6. Lionel Barrymore and Orson Welles.

Chapter Sixteen: The Worst Version

1. "The Night the Reindeer Died."
2. Buddy Hackett(!) plays Scrooge. Former Olympic gymnast Mary-Lou Retton(!!) plays Tiny Tim.
3. A towel and a washcloth.
4. John Forsythe plays Lou Hayward, for-mer network chief.
5. The Ghost of Christmas Past is a cabdriv-er who appears at noon. His license plate reads, "Xmas Past."
6. The Tiny Tim surrogate here is named Calvin. He's a poor black boy who hasn't spoken a word since he witnessed the brutal murder of his father.
7. Bill Murray's full name in this picture is Francis Xavier Cross. You see it on a plaque during the scene where Cross's coffin is cremated. His job is President of the IBC Network. As for his nickname,

Cross's girlfriend Clair (Karen Allen) calls him "Lumpy."

8. Staple them on.

9. A set of twelve Ginzu knives.

10. By socking him in the jaw and literally *knocking* him into the next location!

11. Calvin is watching the 1951 Alastair Sim version of *A Christmas Carol* on his television set. And he sees a closeup of Tiny Tim (Glyn Dearman) exclaiming, "God bless us, every one!"

12. Actually, there are *two* Christmas Future Ghosts here. Or rather, two different versions of the same Spirit. The first one is seen as a huge, menacing figure on a "video wall" over Cross's shoulder; it's draped in black robes and hood, and has the gigantic face of a skull. The second Future Ghost shows up in an elevator with Cross. This one's also robed in black and wears a hood and seems a good eight feet tall. The second Ghost, however, doesn't have a skull for a face. It has a *video monitor* inside its hood instead, which alternately screens the action going on at its feet or shows mutilated representations of Cross's own face! Neither Ghost talks.

13. "Put a Little Love in Your Heart."

ABOUT YE AUTHOR

PAUL MICHAEL SAMMON was born in 1949, in Philadelphia, three days before Christmas.

Perhaps it's the date of his birth. Or the fact that, in 1962, at the age of twelve, he first saw *Mr. Magoo's Christmas Carol* on television. Whatever the reason, Sammon has been haunted by any and all variations of Charles Dickens's holiday fable ever since.

This book is his attempt to lay that particular Christmas Ghost to rest.

Sammon has edited the "extreme horror" anthologies *Splatterpunks 1* and *Splatterpunks 2*. His anthology of "Dead Elvis" stories and essays, *The King Is Dead: Tales of Elvis Post-Mortem*, was published by Delta Books in 1994. He recently contributed the turn-of-the-century novella "The Wedding Party" to *Ghosts*, a 1995 anthology edited by Peter Straub.

Paul M. Sammon has also written much-praised articles on such films as *RoboCop, E.T.*, and *Conan the Barbarian* for publications like *Omni, Cinefex, American Cinematographer*, and the *Los Angeles Times*. But he doesn't only write about motion pictures; since 1980, Sammon has worked on them as well. He was computer graphics supervisor for *RoboCop 2*, provided publicity services for *Platoon, The Addams Family*, and *The Silence of the Lambs*, and has directed dozens of promotional films for all the major studios.

Sammon is currently writing *Future Noir: The Ultimate Blade Runner Book*, for publication in 1995. As he does, he hopes that, someday, somewhere, some enterprising Hollywood mogul will produce a big-budget *science fiction* version of *A Christmas Carol*

Or at least one directed by John Waters.